The Not So Plain and Simple
Life of Samantha Hoffman

The Not So Plain and Simple Life of Samantha Hoffman

Women of God: Lancaster County Book 1

D.L. Stalnaker

Kardee's Angel Publishing

ISBN: 0692514139
ISBN 13: 9780692514139
Library of Congress Control Number: 2015913911
Kardee's Angel Publishing, Tobaccoville, N.C.
Cover Photos provided by IStock and 123 Royalty Free
Cover design by Kardee's Angel Publishing

Other books by D.L. Stalnaker:

Women of God Series:

Book 1
Jobella: A Story of Loss and Redemption
Book 2
Eliza: A Story of Overcoming Limitations
Book 3
Billie: Story of Dedication and Hope
Book 4
From Tragedy to Victory: Zoe's Story
Book 5
Kari: A Story of a Prodigal Daughter
Book 6
Christmas in Clairmonte

Jesus, Me, & Afternoon Tea

Catnip T and Herb

Tea With Grandy Dee

Comfort and Tea: The Grandy Dee Chronicles

Table of Contents

Dedication

To all my friends and family who continue to support me in my writing and to all those who have made the difficult decision to leave all of those closest to them to pursue their dreams in another part of the country or the world, whether it was for a job or to be with their new family in another location. I had to leave my family behind when I went into the service, so I know how hard it can be.

Disclaimer

THIS IS A work of fiction. The places and people are not real. Any resemblance or reference to people either living or dead is purely coincidental.

Acknowledgments

ANY BIBLICAL QUOTES found in this story are from the King James Version of the Bible.

Prologue

WHO WOULD'VE THOUGHT I'd be here today, living in Lancaster County, being the wife of a Mennonite farmer, and actually enjoying the simple and plain life. Not me, that's for sure.

A few years ago I was a teenager getting into all sorts of trouble with my friends in a small town in North Carolina. I almost ended up in jail for stealing and doing drugs. If it wasn't for my father, who happened to be good friends with the judge, I'm sure I would've ended up in jail. I found out later that some of my so-called friends did some time after I left to spend the summer with my great grandmother. I'm sure they were angry with me because I was able to get out of going to jail for doing the same crimes they were accused of.

I was a thoroughly modern teenager, enjoying all of the same things that my friends enjoyed; things like shopping, going to the mall to hang out, and surfing the Internet and Facebook on my computer. I also enjoyed texting and talking for hours on my cell phone, and enjoying all of the other modern conveniences in today's world.

I was popular in school and had my share of boyfriends. Some people even thought I was pretty with my shiny red hair, green eyes, and fair complexion. I loved going to dances and other social occasions at school with my friends. We often hung out after school on most days since both of my parents worked and I really didn't want to go home and be alone. It was then I started getting into a lot of things that I shouldn't have.

That was when my parents started looking at my pattern of behavior and decided they needed to seek an intervention that would steer me away from the way they thought I was headed.

I would find out later from my great grandmother that I wasn't so different from my mom when she was my age. I guess that is why they did what they did for me.

After the incident with the court for shoplifting, my parents decided to send me to live with my great grandmother for the summer. It upset me, at first, to be separated from my family and friends and I really didn't want to spend the summer with a dried up old woman, but I did what I was told to appease them. Besides, if I didn't go, my father was going to go back to the judge and tell him that he changed his mind and wanted me to go to jail just so I would learn my lesson.

So I spent the summer with Grandy Dee, as I affectionately called her, and found that I actually enjoyed it. We had afternoon teas everyday and I learned a lot about my relatives and their history.

I also learned about living on a farm and I had a lot of adventures, including almost dying...twice!

One of the biggest things that happened to me that summer was meeting Benjamin Hoffmann. His family was neighbors with my great grandmother and he often came over to help her with her chores. Over the course of the summer we fell in love and a year later we were married.

Another very large thing that happened in my life that summer was that I became a Christian and joined my Grand and Ben's Mennonite church.

After I left my great grandmother's house at the end of that summer, I was no longer the same wild, uncontrollable teenager I was before I came to stay with her. My friends didn't know what to make of the change in me and most of them didn't want to hang out with me anymore. That was okay by me, I found a new circle of friends with my church family as well as getting closer to my own parents.

Now, I am living several hours away from my mom and dad and decades away from the life I once knew. I no longer have my modern conveniences around me, and to be honest, I don't even miss them. I've fully embraced the plain and simple lifestyle of my husband and his family and I never want to go back.

CHAPTER 1

Summer

I FINALLY GOT around to sorting through some of my boxes of photographs. I had tried to start my scrapbooks several times before, but there was always something to interrupt me. Being a farmer's wife with three small children kept me extremely busy and didn't leave a lot of time for hobbies.

I started getting into scrapbooking a few years before when I was a teenager. While I was spending the summer with my great grandmother, I organized her old photos of her family into albums. They turned out beautiful, if I do say so, and she loved them. I learned a lot about my heritage through working on those albums and through my visits with her over our afternoon teas. Most of the rest of my family's history, I learned through my later visits with the rest of my relatives.

The last time my mother visited us, she brought me photographs from my childhood and teen years. Since I no longer had a computer, she had to download them and print them for me.

My past seemed like a hundred years ago now, as I looked through those old photos.

As I looked at my old school pictures I was horrified when I saw the shock of red curly hair that always seemed to be out of control and my bright green eyes that reminded me of a cat's eyes. I use to be teased relentlessly by the other kids about my hair. They called me all kinds of names and I hated it. As I stared at that picture, I recalled a not so pleasant memory.

One day when I was in first or second grade, I decided to do something about my hair. While my mother was busy entertaining a group of her friends over tea, I snuck into her art studio and got a bottle of her black ink. I had seen my mother dye her hair before, so I thought I'd try it with the ink. I crept quietly into the bathroom and locked the door. I poured the ink over my head and blended it through my hair with my bare hands. Then I tried to wash my hair with shampoo to get rid of the excess. What a mess! There was ink everywhere! My hair was streaked with black, but still had strands of red showing through because I didn't blend it through completely. On top of that, I had black streaks on my face from where the ink dripped down over my skin. My hands and arms were also covered with it. I tried scrubbing my hands and face until they nearly bled but the ink just wouldn't disappear. As I sat on the side of the tub, looking around at the mess I made in the bathroom and on my body, I started to cry.

After my mother's tea with her friends was over, she came upstairs and heard me crying in the bathroom. She knocked on the door and I quickly wrapped a towel around my head before I let her in.

She gasped when she saw me, and the mess I made. "Samantha Ann Edgerton, what in the world have you done!" she yelled.

I started sobbing even harder when she saw me. "I wanted to dye my hair. I'm tired of being picked on because of my red hair!" I said, as I unwrapped the towel from my head.

She tried to soothe me even though she was still angry. "Having red hair is nothing to be ashamed of. Your ancestors were from Ireland and England. Red hair is common over there. You should be proud of it!"

"So how come you color your hair, if you are so proud of it?" I asked.

"I am proud of it, but sometimes women just like to try something different for a change. You are only seven years old for goodness sake, so quit changing the subject. You've made a mess of yourself and this bathroom, young lady, and you're just going to have to live with it! Maybe next time you try something so stupid, you'll think twice about it!"

I was mortified when I went to school the next day. My face and hands were still stained from the ink and my hair was black with red streaks. I looked like a freak, like something out of a horror movie. If I thought I was bullied before, wait until they see me now! I tried to hide myself in shame, as I could feel everyone staring at me and whispering about me.

After about a week, my mother started feeling sorry for me when I came home in tears everyday from school, so finally, she helped me get rid of the stains on my skin. We tried a gritty soap, lemons, baby oil, and finally bleach before it was nearly gone. Then she took me to the hairdresser to see what we could do about my hair. We had been washing it everyday, but it was still jet black in spots. My once beautiful hair had been dried out and damaged from all the washings. The hairdresser had to cut off a lot of my hair to get rid of the damaged ends and then she put a special solution of bleach and peroxide on what was left, to lighten it. After all that, she colored it as close to the original as she could and put a strong conditioner on it. When she was through I looked in the mirror and with the exception of having shorter hair, I looked pretty normal again.

I went back to school the following Monday and all my friends seemed to forget how horrible I looked a few days earlier. They even complimented me on how cute my hair was.

If I looked like that now, the way all these modern teenagers are, I would've fit right in, but there wasn't anything cool about it when I was seven years old. Of course, my mom and dad had to take pictures of me right after it happened so she could further my humiliation for several years down the road. She included those pictures with the ones she gave me. My little girls would get a kick out of seeing how silly their mamma looked, but back then, I was mortified.

Now when I look at the photo, I have to smile. I lived through it and now it's just one of those special childhood memories, something to laugh about and share with my own daughters.

I was so caught up in the memories, I lost track of time.

"What are we having for supper?" Ben asked, coming through the door, carrying baby Matthew on his hip and followed by two very rambunctious little girls trailing after him.

He was interrupted by little Deidre Ann, whom we nicknamed Deedee, named for her great-great grandma. She was carrying a small meowing ball of fur. "Mamma, look what we found in the barn! Isn't it the cutest little kitten?"

"It's darling, Deedee, but I think you need to leave it with its mamma for a little while longer."

"That's the thing, Sam," Ben frowned, "I think the kitten may be lost. There was no sign of a mamma cat anywhere around. It may be an orphan for all we know."

"Can I keep it, Mamma?" she pleaded with me.

I looked into her beautiful sad green eyes as she begged, and then I looked at her father. He grinned and nodded at me.

"No fair, it's two against one," I grinned. "I guess if it's okay with your father, it's okay with me, but it can only stay inside until it gets big enough to take care of itself, understand?"

"Jah, Mamma," she said in unison with her younger sister, Anna, who was trailing behind her.

Ben sat Matthew in his high chair, gave me a quick kiss, and then followed the girls to find a box and some old rags for the kitten's bed. I found an old saucer that could be used for milk.

No sooner had we settled the kitten in her new bed in the utility room then Ben's parents drove up the driveway.

We lived on a farm just about a mile down the road from his folks and they visited us frequently and sometimes without warning. *'It's a gut thing I love his family!'* I thought.

"I made some chicken pot pies today and I'm afraid I made too much and didn't want to waste it. I brought one over for your supper. You didn't have anything planned, did you?" Linda, my mother-in-law, asked.

"Your timing couldn't be more perfect. I absolutely didn't have anything planned. Would you like to join us for supper? I'll cut up a toss salad to go with it."

"That sounds great. We'd love to stay and visit for a little while. By the way, Deidre Ann met us as we drove up. She said that she and her sister found a new kitten."

"Jah, I think Ben and the children are with it in the room just off the kitchen right now."

I put the chicken pie on the counter and covered it with towels to keep it warm while we went to check on the kitten.

The kitten was a calico cat with long fur and couldn't have been much more than two weeks old. It had a white face and belly and paws. I had to admit that she was beautiful.

"What are you going to name her?" John asked.

"How do you know it's a her?" Deedee asked her dawdy.

"Well, it is a calico cat, and most calico cats are girls."

"She looks like she has mittens on her feet. Can I call her Mittens, Dat?"

"That name does suit her, sweetie. If your sister agrees with it, Mittens it is."

As we were all in the utility room admiring the kitten, we heard a loud crash coming from the kitchen. We all ran to the kitchen to find Ginger, our golden retriever, licking up the chicken pie from the floor. We shooed her away from it and ran her back outside, through the door that someone had left open. We worried about the possibility of her accidently eating a piece of broken glass with the food, as the casserole dish was shattered amongst the food.

Ginger was one of the offspring of my great grandmother's golden retriever. Her dog passed away shortly after she died. The dog was aging and was brokenhearted after her master died and she didn't live long after my great grandmother's death. We couldn't bear to part with Ginger, so when we took over her farm, Ginger was naturally a part of it. Somehow having her around reminded me of Grandy Dee and her old sidekick.

We would have to watch her closely over the next few days to make sure she didn't accidently swallow some broken glass and cause damage to her stomach or intestines.

After I cleaned up the mess, I realized that I didn't have anything else prepared to cook. I was going to fix a salad to go along with the pie, but that wasn't going to be filling enough for the hungry brood that would be gathered around my table.

"I still have the pie I made for us at our house. If you want to go ahead with the salad, you can bring that and come and eat with us," Linda suggested.

"Are you sure you can handle all of us?" I asked.

"You know you all are welcome anytime," John smiled.

They left to go back home and after I cleaned up the rest of the mess and made the salad, we piled the kinner into the van and headed to their house.

The children loved to go to their grandparent's house. They liked playing in the gazebo that John and Ben had built for our wedding reception over six years ago. It remained a permanent fixture on their property and now, every time I visit, I'm reminded of that wonderful day. When we weren't using it for our outdoor picnics, the children liked to use it as their own private playhouse.

Ben and I were sitting on the porch, taking turns holding our one-year-old son, Matthew, who we affectionately called Mattie, while we were watching the girls play in the front yard.

"Supper is served," Linda called from the kitchen.

She didn't have to call twice. We were all famished by the time we got ready to eat. We gathered around the large kitchen table and held hands to pray. As the head of the house and family, John said the blessing.

"Our Heavenly Father, for this food we are about to eat, we are truly thankful. Thank you for those who are gathered here and bless and care for these little ones you have blessed us with. Bless this food to our bodies and our bodies to your service. In Jesus most precious name, amen."

Then Deedee spoke up before lifting her head, "And Jesus, please bless Ginger and Mittens too. Amen"

"Amen," we echoed and I gave her hand a squeeze. Deedee had always been tenderhearted when it came to animals. Sometimes that tenderness would be a problem when it came time to kill some of the farm animals for meat. She took after me in that respect. As a former city girl, this was the hardest thing for me to accept when I became a farmer's wife. I was use to my family buying meat from the grocery store. Although I knew it came from animals, I never gave it a second thought until I lived on a farm and ate what we raised ourselves. I still can't bring myself to kill anything, so I leave that to the menfolk. I only recently could bring myself to pluck and skin the chickens. We tried to shelter the children from the sight of the slaughter. They would be exposed to it soon enough. In the meantime, as far as they knew, the meat came from the store.

Linda's chicken pie was delicious and there was plenty enough to go around, but there was nothing left over. She had made a pound cake for dessert and we ate some fresh strawberries and cream on top of it.

We sat on the front porch after supper and had a cup of coffee and visited while the girls continued to play in the yard. Matthew was too young to crawl around in the grass, so we took turns holding him while we talked.

Beyond the gazebo, there was a lovely little pond. It was a beautiful view, especially as the sun was setting. The gold, red, and violet of the sunset reflected brilliantly on the surface of the water. What a nice painting it would be if one were to stop and capture its beauty.

Baby Matthew, began to get fussy as I tried to hold him and I knew that it was time to get all the kinner home and get them to bed. We also needed to get back to check on Mittens and Ginger to make sure they weren't getting into any mischief.

When we arrived home, the first thing Deedee and Anna did was to run to the utility room to see Mittens.

I heard squealing and ran to see what was the matter, fearing that the kitten was dead or something.

"Mamma, Mittens is gone!" cried Anna.

I pulled both of the girls into my arms. "Don't worry girls, she couldn't have gotten too far. Did you close the door behind you when you came out of the room earlier?"

"I'm not sure, Mamma," Deedee said, with tears in her eyes.

"Well, let me get Matthew changed and put to bed and then I'll help you look for her. In the meantime, maybe your dat can help you look, jah?"

About that same time, Ben came into the house, frowning. "Sam, I think we better keep an eye on Ginger. She's not acting right. She's laying down and barely moved when I called to her."

"We have a problem in here as well. Mittens is missing and the girls are frantic. Can you help them look for her while I change Matthew and put him to bed? After I get him down, I will help you with both the animals."

By the time I got Matthew finally settled down, I went into the kitchen and found Ben and the girls sitting at the table with Mittens in the center of them lapping up a saucer of milk.

"Where was she?" I asked.

"She was curled up behind the washing machine. I didn't think we'd ever get her out of there. She was covered in lint and we had to give her a good brushing."

"She could probably use a good bath as well," I added.

"Well, we can worry about doing that tomorrow. I'm anxious to go find out what's going on with Ginger right now. Can you get the girls ready for bed while I'm checking on her?"

"Sure, no problem. I was going to do that anyway."

"Mamma, is Ginger going to be okay?" Anna asked, with tears in her eyes.

"I'm sure of it, sweetie."

"Can Mittens sleep in our room tonight, please???" added Deedee.

"As long as you keep her in the box, I don't see any reason why you can't. She's not to get in your bed, though, and we need to find a box with taller sides so she can't get out."

"I've got a larger box in the storage shed that would keep her contained better," Ben suggested.

After I got the children all bedded down for the night, along with the kitten, I joined Ben as he was examining Ginger. We were both concerned for her. As she lay there, I noticed that her abdomen was swollen. I had never noticed it before and wondered if this was something new. The first thing I thought of was that she could be bleeding internally. Did she swallow a piece of broken glass when she got into that pie?

Then I saw the bleeding coming from her bottom. This was serious! I started getting nervous when she started getting restless and aggressive as we patted her abdomen.

"I'm taking her to the animal hospital emergency room, Sam. She's just not doing right. I'm worried about her. If we don't do something, she may be gone by morning."

I fully trusted Ben and his feelings about the dog. He had great instincts when it came to his animals. He had even started taking some vet classes at the local university. He hoped to become a full-fledged veterinarian in a few years.

After he left, and the children were fast asleep, I made myself a cup of chamomile tea and sat and read my Bible. I tried to stay awake so I would be up when he came back home, but the stress and busyness of the day took its toll and I drifted off to sleep, curled up on my bed with my quilt wrapped snuggly around me.

I woke up the next morning to the full sunlight and the roosters in the yard making their usual early dawn racket. I ran to the window to see if Ben had made it home yet, but his truck was nowhere to be found.

CHAPTER 2

I CHECKED ON the children and their kitten and all of them were sound asleep, so I decided to get dressed and go outside to feed the animals and gather the eggs. I would milk the cows after breakfast after everyone was awake.

I was worried about Ben not returning home. It brought back memories of the summer when we met. One horrible day that summer, he didn't return home after we had gone out on a date. No one had heard from him for days. We later learned that he had been kidnapped and his truck was stolen and he was left for dead. When he finally did show up he was naked and had severe bruises from where he had been beaten up. Thankfully they had caught the man who did it and he was later sentenced to twenty years in prison for what he had done.

While I was feeding the horses their oats, Deedee came out on the porch in her nightgown and carrying Mittens.

"Deidre Ann, you better get back inside with your kitten before she gets away from you," I fussed at her.

She looked around. "Where are Dat and Ginger?"

"They haven't returned home from the doctor yet."

"I'm hungry," she pleaded.

"Let me finish here and I'll be right there to get you some breakfast."

"Mommy, Mattie is crying. He woke up Anna and me."

"Okay, sweetie, I'm finished now. I'll be right there."

About the time I was closing the gate to the barn, Ben pulled up in this truck. I was concerned when he didn't have Ginger with him.

"What's happened to Ginger?" I gasped, afraid of the worst. "Where is she?"

"She's going to stay at the vet's for a couple of days. He was concerned that she did may have swallowed some glass and wants to watch her and monitor her bowel movements for a day or two. Sam they did a sonogram on her to check for internal bleeding, but they didn't find anything. But what they did find may surprise you. It seems that Ginger is pregnant! They found four pups when they scanned her."

"How far along is she?"

"He estimated about a month. As long as the other problem is solved, she should be fine."

"Do we tell the children?"

"Let's wait until she is out of woods and all right. We can tell them when she gets home, jah?"

"I'll bet you're hungry and exhausted after the long night."

"I managed to sleep some in the waiting room, but I could use some breakfast and a short nap before I get to work."

I got the children up and dressed and Matthew taken care of and cooked their breakfast. Matthew continued to be a little fussy, so I took the children outside and played with them so Ben could get some uninterrupted sleep. As I headed towards the door, the phone rang. I quickly answered it and took it outside with me, so it wouldn't bother my husband. It was his mamm.

"What's the word with Ginger?" she asked.

"The vet's going to keep her a couple of days to keep an eye on her until the possible danger of broken glass is passed. Linda, Ginger is pregnant with four pups, can you believe it?" I spoke quietly, so the girls wouldn't hear that last part.

"How did that happen? She hasn't been around any other dog has she?"

"Not as far as I know, but obviously she has. There must have been some strays around that we didn't know about. Ben just got home a little while ago. He stayed at the vet's all night with her."

"I'll bet he's exhausted. Do you need any help at your place today?"

"No, I've already fed the animals and gathered the eggs. Ben said he was able to get some sleep at the doctor's and felt like he'd be good as new after a short nap. I just need to keep the children quiet so he can rest. It won't be easy, though, Matthew is really fussy today. I think he may be teething or something. He's running a little bit of a fever."

"I thought he felt a little warm last night. I hope that is all that's wrong with him. You might want to put a little ice on his gums and see if that makes him feel better and give him something to chew on."

"I'll try that, I know it certainly worked with the girls."

It didn't take long before the children and I got tired of being outside. It was hot, and Mattie was growing more irritable, so we decided to go back inside where it was cooler. The girls were anxious to get back to playing with Mittens and I warned them to play quietly while their dat slept. I decided to try giving some ice to the baby and then give him a bath to see if it would calm him down.

When I was undressing him I noticed a rash on his face that was slowly spreading to his stomach and back, but I didn't think too much of it. We had been outside in the heat, so I figured it was just a heat rash. He was feeling a little warm, so I took his temperature again. I was surprised when I learned that it was over one hundred and two degrees. I quickly dipped him in some cool water to bring his temperature down and hopefully reverse the heat rash that seemed to be spreading. When he began shivering, I quickly removed him from the water and bundled him up in some warm towels and ran to wake Ben.

"Maybe we'd better call my mamm and see if she can give us some advice on this one. I don't believe that teething would cause all of this."

"I talked to her a little while ago, but that was before I saw how high his temperature was."

So I called Linda and told her what was happening, and she agreed with Ben. She and John came to the house and she took one look at him and said that we needed to get him to the doctor right away. They said they'd take the girls to their house and take care of them while we were gone.

It was on a Saturday and I was worried about whether we would find a clinic open that day. We didn't have any insurance and had to rely on a local doctor in town that catered to the needs of the Amish and Mennonite community and offered services that could be paid over time. We called ahead and they said that they would only be open until noon, but they would try to see him, if we got him there as soon as possible.

On our way to the doctor's office, I had Mattie bundled up, but he was still shivering like he was freezing to death. By the time we got to the office, he was quiet and difficult to arouse.

When we rushed into the waiting area, the receptionist took one look at him and immediately had us take him back to the examination room. When the nurse and doctor entered the room they were wearing masks, gowns, and gloves. Mattie looked terrified when he saw them dressed like that and started crying. My heart was breaking for my little boy. He looked miserable. Besides the rash, his eyes were red and watery, and his nose was runny. I just figured it was from his crying. The nurse took his temperature and it had gone up to over one hundred and three. They immediately started cool water baths and started an IV of saline because he had become so dehydrated from being so hot. They also gave him a fever reducing, pain medication in his IV.

When the doctor was through examining him, he turned to me, "Mrs. Hoffmann, by all indications and the symptoms he's exhibiting it looks like Matthew has the measles. Has he been vaccinated against it?"

"No, I felt he was just too young. He just turned one and I was going to wait until he was at least eighteen months old."

"Well, he should have had it done sooner than this, but it's water under the bridge now. Have the two of you been vaccinated? What about your other children?"

"I had it done when I was a young girl. My mom believed in all that stuff. Our girls had their initial vaccines when they were younger, but we didn't get them back for their boosters," I replied.

Ben added, "I was never vaccinated, but when I was little I had something that my mamm thought was the measles. She never took me to the doctor for it though, so I'm not sure if that's what it was for certain."

"Mrs. Hoffman, between you and your husband, you should be the one to take care of the baby. You probably have the best resistance since you have been vaccinated. Mr. Hoffman, without knowing your medical history, I have no way of determining if you have a resistance or not. You would be better off having limited contact with your son. Above all, keep your girls away from him. Without getting their boosters, their immunity may not be complete. Actually, it wouldn't hurt for each of you to get a booster shot, even now."

"What else can I give him? Is there medicine for it?"

"No antibiotics will help, because it is a virus, but what you can give him is some baby Tylenol for his fever and make sure he drinks plenty of fluids, and keep him cooled down as much as possible. The fever is the most dangerous thing along with dehydration. All of his symptoms should go away in a week to ten days. If his temperature gets worse or he starts having seizures or breathing difficulties get him to the emergency room immediately. I don't want to worry you too much, but measles in someone this young is a very serious illness. You need to stay with him and treat him continually. Remember this illness is extremely contagious, so keep him separated from the rest of the family. Make sure his room, bedding, and clothing is kept clean and sanitary. Don't let anyone touch anything that he has been around and make sure you wash your hands frequently."

When we arrived back at the house, Ben called his parents and told them what was wrong and asked them if they would keep the girls for the next few days to keep them safe.

Of course, they agreed. They even agreed to let Mittens come too, so she could keep the girls company.

Since I had been handling Matthew, Ben packed the girls things and loaded their bags and Mittens in the back of the truck and headed to his parents house.

I changed the linens in Mattie's crib and changed his clothes. He was drenched from sweating as his fever came down from the medication the doctor gave him. I took the time to prepare him several bottles of juice and breast milk, so I could give him plenty of fluids. I kept a basin of cool water and towels in his room, so I could sponge him off once in a while.

Just as I had finally settled him down enough for him to rest, Ben came back home. His mother sent a casserole back with him and he made a pitcher of lemonade to go with it. He brought it in Mattie's room, but I warned him about getting to close to us. Still, he couldn't resist the temptation to come over to us and kiss my top of my head before saying goodnight. He glanced at Mattie and then before leaving, he said a prayer for his recovery and our safety over the next few days.

I was pleased when he came back to the room a little while later with a couple of quilts and a pillow and a clean night gown and change of clothes for me. What a thoughtful and loving husband I had. God had blessed me with a wonderful man when I married Benjamin Hoffmann six years ago.

Mattie finally was resting and his temperature had finally come down enough to allow him to sleep. I made a pallet on the floor with the quilts and changed into my nightgown.

I had undone the bun in my hair and combed out my long red tresses and put them in a loose braid for the night. Having long hair was something I had to get use to when I joined the Old Order Mennonite church that my husband belonged to. Wearing long dresses all of the time was another thing I wasn't use to, but after six years, it had become second nature to me and I never even missed my jeans and long pants anymore.

It was hard for me to fall asleep. The floor was hard even with the quilts, but the thing that kept me awake was worrying about my baby bu. I was extremely tired, but I worried that he would wake up with a raging fever again and become distressed.

So as I lay there, I thought back to the first time I met his father and fell in love:

I had come to live with my great grandmother, Grandy Dee, for the summer. I was in some trouble for doing drugs and shoplifting back home. Rather than going to jail for a time, my dad convinced the judge, who also happened to be his best friend, to give me another chance. So their idea of punishment was to send me to live with my great grandmother for a few months. It would get me away from my so-called friends for a while, as well as teach me some life lessons, and since my Grand was almost a hundred years old, I would be a welcomed and much needed help for her on the farm.

I wasn't looking forward to being away from home for so long and away from my friends, but the alternative was if I stayed at home, I'd have to put up with the continual condemnation of my parents and the very real threat of jail time, if I got into trouble again.

So we made the eight-hour trip to Pennsylvania and Lancaster county from North Carolina. It was a pleasant enough drive as we took the scenic route as we made our way north. I enjoyed the scenery along the way, that is, when I wasn't sleeping in the back seat listening to my IPod.

When we finally got to her house, I was surprised at the quaint old farmhouse. It was actually quite charming with its fanciful gingerbread trim. It kind of looked like a dollhouse.

I had never been on a farm before, except when I was very little and we had visited her. The only animals I had ever gotten close to were at the state fair in Raleigh, so I was a little intimidated by them at first, especially the larger ones. I didn't know if I'd ever get use to them.

After my parents left and I was alone with Grandy Dee, I had to either warm up to my new situation or suffer for the rest of the summer, but warming up to her was easier than I thought it would be. Soon she was having me help her feed the chickens and gather their eggs, and feed some of the other animals. Thankfully, she milked the cows. I didn't know if I'd ever be ready to do that.

A couple of days after I arrived, I met Benjamin Hoffman. He lived at the next farm over from hers and he came over to help her out with some of her heavier chores a couple of times a week.

He was nineteen years old at the time, and two years older than me. When I first saw him that first day, walking up her path, I couldn't believe how handsome he was. I suddenly believed that this summer was going to be much better that I thought it would be.

Over the next three months and several adventures later, we fell in love and by the time our summer had come to an end, our courtship was getting serious.

When I left that summer, I was getting ready to turn eighteen and I was engaged. My parents weren't too thrilled that it happened so quickly and I still had another year of high school left, but we didn't have any plans to be married until the following summer after I graduated and I guess they thought that with our being separated for almost a year, it would end the relationship. They had said that if we still felt the same by then, they would give their blessings to us.

Being separated over the next several months was difficult, but we wrote almost every day and called at least once a week. When Christmas vacation came, his family came to North Carolina to visit. Ben's step-sister, Kari, and her family lived nearby, so when they came to see her, they also spent some time with my family and me.

As I was thinking about that first summer, I slowly drifted off to sleep. Just as I finally was able to rest, Mattie woke up screaming. Ben came running into the room, as I was getting up to tend to him.

"What's going on? Is the baby okay?"

"I was just getting ready to check on him. He had finally fallen asleep and I was resting my eyes a bit. He just now woke up again."

"I wish I could relieve you so you could get some rest."

"No, it's okay. I can't take a chance on you getting sick, as well."

After he left out of the room, I picked the baby up. He was burning up with fever again. I went through the steps again to bring down his fever. I gave him his Tylenol, wrapped him in cool wet towels and fed him some cool juice and held him until he quieted down again. While I was undressing him, I noted that his entire body was covered with the rash now. It made me sad to see my little one so miserable. I just prayed that the rest of my family didn't get this illness. I hoped that they had enough immunity to protect them.

When he began to feel cooler again and fell back to sleep, I attempted to lay down again to rest. I tried to soothe myself with more pleasant memories from the past. This time, I thought of the teas that Grandy Dee and I shared during the summer we were together.

Those were pleasant times. No matter how busy we were each day, we always took the time in the afternoon to have a break. We would get out a pretty teacup and some kind of sweets, and sit and visit over a cup of tea. Then she would tell me stories of her life. I hoped when my girls got a little older, I would be able to share her stories with them as well as our own.

As I was thinking about the teacups, I remembered how I had once thought about starting my own tearoom. Somehow through the busyness of farm life and being a wife and mother of three children, those plans had to be put on the back burner for a while. Maybe I would think about it again some day. At least I had a good supply of cups, since Grand left me all of her collection.

I thought about Kari, Ben's stepsister, and her tearoom back in North Carolina. What I wouldn't give to have a place like that.

As I thought of Kari and my family back home, it seemed like a whole other world from what I knew now.

Matthew had finally quieted down to sleep and as I listened to his steady breaths signifying that he was resting comfortably, I was finally able to relax enough to fall asleep.

CHAPTER 3

I WOKE UP with a start when I heard the rooster crowing and the screen door slamming downstairs. Matthew was still asleep when I peeked at him. He was almost too quiet. How long have I been asleep and why had he not awoken?

I felt his forehead and he was burning up with fever. I put him the cooling towels on him but he didn't wake up. He didn't even move!

I tried to give him medicine but I couldn't get him to open his mouth. I tried yelling at him, but no response.

"Ben," I screamed down the stairs, but there was no answer. He must have been out in the barn with the animals. I quickly opened the window to call for him, but I didn't see him anywhere. His truck was gone.

I quickly telephoned his parents. After several rings, Linda finally answered. By this time I was frantic.

"Linda, do you know where Ben went?"

"I believe he went to the vet's office to pick up Ginger. You sound upset, is anything the matter?"

"It's Mattie, I can't wake him up! I tried screaming at him, and trying to make him take some medicine and cooling him with wet towels. Nothing does any good. On top of that he's burning up with fever! It's almost one hundred and six."

"Oh my goodness, I'll get John over there right away. You need to get him to the hospital quickly. In the meantime keep trying to cool him down with the towels and force the medicine in his mouth, even if he's not swallowing, he'll get some of it. I'll keep the girls here while you and John are gone."

Before we hung up, I heard John walk into her house and she was telling him what happened. I heard him rush out the door as we ended our conversation.

"My prayers go with you sweet girl and with my precious grandson. We'll let Ben know what happened when he gets home. I'm sure he'll be there as soon as possible. God be with you both."

I quickly dressed and continued to do what I could to arouse Matthew and bring down his temperature while we were waiting for his dawdy John.

We were both waiting for him on the porch when he pulled into the driveway in his black van.

He took one look at Mattie, and knew that there wasn't any more time to lose.

We rushed to the hospital and John was speeding most of the way. I just prayed that there were no police around, or many Amish buggies on the road, or worse still, that we wouldn't get in a wreck on the way.

Thankfully, we got to the ER in one piece without a problem.

When the nurses saw my little baby and the condition he was in, they took us back to the exam room immediately and when I told them that he had the measles, they put on their protective clothing before handling him.

They took his temperature. It had come down to one hundred and four, but that was still dangerously high and he was still unresponsive. They started an IV and began giving him medicine to bring down the fever and began sponging him off with ice water. When the doctor came in, he examined him thoroughly and tested his reflexes. Nothing. He forced his eyes open and checked for pupil response to light. Again there was no response.

While the nurses were watching over him, the doctor pulled me aside. "Mrs. Hoffman, I'm afraid that your baby is in a very bad way. It appears that he more than likely has some brain swelling from the high fever and the measles. He is in a coma right now. That is why he's not waking up. We will need to keep him in the hospital and watch him. They will work around the clock to bring his temperature under control and monitor him for any signs of brain damage while he tries to wake up. We will give him medication in his IV's. He will get anti-viral medication, as well as fever reducing medicine. We are also going to put in a nasogastric tube down through his nose to feed him, and I'm afraid that he will also need to be put on a ventilator so we can make sure he gets the oxygen he needs. Right now his breathing is very shallow and he's not getting enough air to sustain him."

"What are we going to do? We can't afford all this. We don't have any insurance," I sobbed.

John, who was standing next to me, put his arms around me. "Don't you worry about anything, Samantha, the Lord will provide. We must do this for your boy. I'll guarantee the hospital bill, and the Lord will do the rest."

I turned back to the doctor. "Is it alright if I stay with my baby?"

"I was going to suggest that. You can stay as long as you like, as long as you realize that when the nurses are caring for him, you'll have to leave them to do their jobs. You'll also have to wear protective gear while you're with him and if you leave his room to go somewhere else in the hospital, you'll have to stay away from others. We don't need a measles epidemic, for goodness sake. Little Matthew will be on an isolation ward while he is here, at least until he is no longer contagious."

"I understand."

After he was admitted and we were settled into a room, Mattie was hooked up to the nasogastric tube feeding and the ventilator and had monitor leads attached to his head and chest. I sat in the corner of the room praying and reading the Bible that was left in the bedside table by the Gideon's, but it was hard for me to concentrate.

John turned to me before he left. "Keep praying and reading your Bible, Samantha. That is the best thing you can do for little Mattie right now. I'm going to leave you now. I'm sure Linda is worried sick by this time and I need to get home and let her know what's happening. I'm just in the way here, anyways. Don't lose your faith, sweet girl. God will take care of this, no matter what happens. When I see Ben I'll make sure he gets here as soon as possible. Don't worry about your girls. They can stay with us as long as it takes."

As he turned to go, Ben came rushing past him into the room and grabbed me up into his arms.

"Ben, you shouldn't be touching me," I cried. "I've been handling our boppli. I could be contagious."

"I don't care, I need to hold you now and we need to comfort one another. If I were to get the measles, so be it."

"You don't mean that! What would I do if you were to get sick too?"

"If I were going to get sick, I would have started getting symptoms by now."

"I'm surprised that the nurses let you in without a gown on."

"I was in such a rush to get in here, I don't think they even noticed me!"

About that time one of the nurses came in with a stern look on her face and a gown, gloves, and a mask in her hand for him to put on. "You can't be too careful, Mr. Hoffmann. You need to put these on," the nurse commanded. "Especially before touching your son. We need to protect him as well as you."

After he put the protective gear on he walked over to the crib where Mattie was still deep in his coma. He laid his hand on the baby's abdomen and kissed his forehead. "You'd better quit laying around, son, I'm going to be needing your help in the back forty. I can't get it plowed up without your help," he frowned. "Get well soon. Mattie, your mom and I love you and need you." He kissed him again through his mask and turned to me. The tears were flowing down his face by now, and as we held each other we could feel each other's body shake with our sobs.

When our emotions were finally under control, I remembered that he had gone to the vet's that morning. It was nice to be able to change the subject for a few moments.

"I almost forgot, how is Ginger doing? Did you get to bring her home today?"

"Yes, she's home, and getting bigger by the day. She's gotten lazy with her pregnancy. She's going to be totally useless by the time she has her pups. The vet thinks that the danger of the glass is over and has given her a clean bill of health."

"I totally know how she feels being pregnant. If you remember I got a little lazy myself with each of our children."

"I remember, I had to do everything around the house by the end of each of your pregnancies, especially when you were pregnant with Matthew. Anna was two and Deidre was three and they kept me very busy!"

At the mention of Matthew, a dark cloud fell over me again. I couldn't bear it, if something bad happened to him. Would Ben blame me for not watching him as carefully as I should have last night? Could I have prevented this from happening?

"What's the matter, Sam?" he asked when he saw me frowning again.

"Oh Ben, I'm so sorry I didn't watch Mattie closer. It's all my fault he's here today."

"Samantha, I don't blame you. You did the best you could. This is just a horrible disease and you were exhausted from caring for him. I should have stepped in and helped so you could get some rest. Please don't be so hard on yourself."

"Still, I'll never forgive myself if he doesn't get better."

"Look, sweetie, I don't really want to leave you but I need to get back to the farm to do some chores. I'll call your folks when I get there and let them know what's happening, and then I'll be back later and bring some clean clothes and toiletries for you. Is there anything else you need? Do you need money for food?"

"No, they are bringing trays for me at meal time. To tell you the truth, I've kind of lost my appetite since Mattie became so ill."

"You need to keep your strength up. Promise me you'll take care of yourself. I don't want to worry about you too."

"I promise. You'd better go now so you can get some things done. I'll be all right. Give the girls my love and tell them I miss them. Just don't tell them how bad things look for Mattie. I don't want them to worry."

"I will. I love you and I will keep you both in my prayers."

"Same here," he kissed me goodbye and gave Mattie one last kiss before leaving.

I walked over to Mattie's hospital crib. He looked so sweet and peaceful as he lay there. I was comforted by the steady beeps from the heart monitor and the pulse oximeter that was recording his oxygen levels. Everything looked normal from what I could tell. His brain monitor was also showing normal fluctuations according to the nurse. She said that was a good sign and it gave me hope. He had a temperature probe stuck to his forehead that recorded his current temperature. I looked at it and his temperature was down to one hundred and one. It wasn't perfect but it was better than what it was when we brought him in.

I was just about to curl up on the recliner in the room to take a nap, when the nurse brought me a meal tray. I started to tell her to take it away, but I thought about what Ben said. I needed to eat something. My baby would need me to be strong for him.

"Thank you."

"I brought a few magazines for you to look at, too, if you're interested. I'm not sure what kind of things your people like to read about."

"Well, I'm not into fashion or celebrities, but I do like to look at gardening or cooking magazines and anything to do with our local culture."

"There is a library on the second floor. Visitors can borrow books and magazines from there too, if you're interested."

"Denki, I mainly read the Bible, but sometimes I enjoy a nice Christian book. I may venture out later to check it out."

"Just let us know when you leave, so we can keep an eye on your son."

"Will do."

I settled down enough to eat a little bit of my lunch. I still wasn't hungry and I piddled with my food. I ate part of it, but I was thankful for the iced tea and the milk. I was thirstier than I realized.

One of the magazines she loaned me was about tea parties. I enjoyed looking at the beautiful china and the recipes for the wonderful snacks. I recognized some of the teacups. There were a few that my great grandmother had. Well, I should say that I have, since she handed them down to me. It made me want to start my own tearoom all over again. It would have to be something I'd have to get permission from the church elders to do, but I think as long as I stayed within the guidelines of our religion, it wouldn't be too much of a problem. Of course, I'd also have to have the blessing of my husband and his family and then, of course, it would be the matter of the money, something that we would surely be short on after paying for the hospital and doctor's bills for Mattie's illness.

I sighed, knowing that it was all just a dream and would probably never happen. As I started to flip the magazine closed one of the ads in the back caught my eye. There, as clear as anything, was an ad for Kari's Southern Tea Room. I wasn't sure if it was my sister-in-law's place, but on further examination of the ad, I found out that it was. I was so proud of her. The ad was beautiful and it looked like she was prospering. There was a link to an article in the previous month's magazine about her place. I would have to check the library or nurses' station to see if they had a copy of that particular magazine anywhere around.

I would ask the nurse when she returned to check on Mattie and pick up my lunch tray.

I walked over to the baby and touched his soft skin. I sang to him an Amish lullaby as I caressed him. His heart rate began to slow down ever so slightly as his brain waves started fluctuating more. Was he responding to my touch and voice? Maybe that was a good sign. I would ask the doctor about that when I saw him again.

I sat back down in the recliner and started reading the Bible. The sounds of all the monitors and the ventilator lulled me to sleep.

Because of looking at the tea magazine and seeing Kari's ad, I dreamt of my last year at home and my time working in her tearoom:

My friends and family couldn't get over the changes that had happened to me over the summer. In my association with Grandy Dee and Ben, I had found God and the Mennonite faith. I had begun thinking and dressing like them, as well as worshiping God, something totally foreign to my way of life before. No one knew quite how to take me, including my parents. My mom understood, of course, since she had grown up around Grand and others of like faith, but my dad wasn't sure if he liked the change in me. When my mom left her home, she threw off the trappings of her religion to join my father in his modern lifestyle.

The kids at school were even less supportive. When I came to school in my long dresses and prayer kapp, and bringing my Bible everywhere I went, they looked at me like I was some kind of freak. I totally ignored them. Their disapproval was no longer a concern to me. Especially since they were the ones who got me into trouble to start with.

I made new friends at the local Mennonite church I started going to on Sundays. Sometimes, I even got my parents to come with me. It was a small congregation, but everyone was very close knit and became like family to me. They helped me to grow in my faith, as I learned more about what it would be like to be married into a Mennonite family.

My other best friend I made was Kari. She was the stepsister of my Ben. Her mother, Linda, whom she had been estranged from several years ago, had met John, Ben's father, and had fallen in love with him. They were living in Washington State at the time, having moved there following the death of Ben's mother. After they were married, the three of them moved back to his farm in Pennsylvania, the farm that was just down the road from my Grand's.

To make a long story short, Kari and Linda eventually found one another again. Kari was happy to have found her mother and was able to ask for her forgiveness, and Linda was thrilled that she was not only reunited with her, but also learned that she was a grandmother to two wonderful children.

Kari had a real nice tearoom and I had visited it whenever I could. It reminded me of my afternoon teas with Grand. Kari and I would chat when she wasn't too busy with other customers. Being with her made me feel closer to her brother.

After a couple of months, she asked me if I would like to come to work there at the tearoom part time. I was thrilled for the opportunity. It would give me a chance to earn a little money, as well as get the experience of running my own one day. I had thought about opening a tearoom of my own someday, as long as it was allowed after Ben and I were married.

At Christmastime, Ben and his family came to visit Kari and her family. When I wasn't working, I spent a lot of time with them. I was glad I was out of school for winter break when they were in North Carolina. It was nice to be able to go to church where I could introduce my boyfriend and his family to my friends. My parents and Kari's family came with us the Sunday of their special Christmas service. It was wonderful to have all of the people I loved in one place worshipping our God.

For Christmas, Ben surprised me with an engagement ring. It wasn't anything fancy and I would've been just as happy with the promise ring he bought for me that summer, but it was a symbol that we truly were engaged now and I couldn't be happier.

As we talked about the wedding we would have the next summer, we decided that Kari and her husband, Jacob, would stand up with us as matron of honor and best man. Their children, Aiden and Laurie, would be the ring bearer and flower girl. We would be married in Ben's church. I wanted to have it there so my great grandmother could attend. It was really important to me to have her there. I figured my parents could also stop in Virginia on their way to Pennsylvania for the wedding, to pick up my grandmother, Anna, at the nursing home in Richmond. It would be great to see her again.

After Ben and his parents left to go back home, it was back to school and my job again. Every night I prayed that the time would pass by quickly until we could be together again.

"Mrs. Hoffman, wake up, your husband is here. I also found the magazine you were looking for. Hope you enjoy the article on your sister-in-law's tearoom. I took the time to read it after you mentioned it. It was very inspirational. "

Ben came in dressed in the isolation gear he had to put on.

"The nurse said you were finally able to get a nap. I hated to wake you up. Did you sleep well?"

"Jah, it was a nice nap."

"I brought you some things from the house so you could freshen up a bit."

"Denki, I could use a good bath. Maybe I'll get a shower tonight."

"The girls made you and Mattie cards. We all miss you very much. We'll be so happy to have you both home again."

"Me too. This is no fun for me either."

He walked over to the crib to look at Mattie. "It might be my imagination, but his rash looks lighter now."

"I noticed that too, but it may just be the lighting in this room and the reflection of all the monitors on him."

Later that evening after Ben left, my parents called to see how we were coping. Things had happened so quickly earlier in the day that I didn't even think to call them, although Ben said he'd call when he got back to the house.

"I'm so sorry I didn't call and let you know about Mattie sooner. He's been ever so ill over the last two days and now he's in a coma and on life support in the hospital. I'm scared Mamma. I don't want anything to happen to my beautiful boy," I cried.

"Ben called us and told us what happened. Are you able to stay with him?"

"Jah, there's a recliner in the room and Ben brought some clean clothes and a night gown for me. The nurses and doctors have been great and very supportive towards us."

"Not to stress you further, but how are you all going to pay for his care?"

"I'm trying not to think of that. Right now, I can only be concerned about my baby. I'm trusting the Lord to take care of him and all the financial details."

"We'd like to help you all out with that."

"Denki, but we don't want to take your money. Gott will provide."

"We want to help, Matthew is our grandson and you are still our daughter. Besides, one of the ways that God provides is to lay it on people's hearts to give where they can."

"We can talk about it later, Mamma."

"How is he doing?"

"He's still not responding and he is on a ventilator and has IVs and tube feedings, but he seems to be stabilized. His temperature has starting coming down some. The doctor is hopeful that once it stays down and the measles runs its course, that the swelling his brain will also go down."

"We'll be praying that it will happen soon."

"Denki, Mamma. I'll get Ben to call you if there are any changes."

After she hung up, the nurse came in to check on Mattie and give him a bath. She was very gentle with him, but it hurt me to see them with all of their protective gear on to prevent them from spreading his illness to the others on the unit. I understood their reasons, but it made me feel like we were outcasts in an alien world.

When supper was over, I asked the nurse if I could leave him long enough to take a quick shower and she said that it wouldn't be a problem. They would keep an eye out for him while I was in the bathroom. She brought in some extra towels and a washcloth for me.

I was thankful for the short reprieve. It felt good to take my hair out of my long braid and to wash my hair. The warm water felt refreshing as I let it soak into every pore of my skin. It was the first good bath I had in several days and it felt wonderful.

I dried off and put on a clean dress and wrapped my wet hair in a towel and walked back into the room, just in time for my in-laws to show up.

"Hi, Samantha! We wanted to come and visit with you and our little boppli."

"Denki for coming. You'll have to excuse the way I look, I was finally able to get a bath and it felt so nice to get clean for a change."

"No problem, you do look refreshed. We wanted to come and have prayer over Mattie and you."

"Denki, all prayers are most certainly welcomed right now. How are Anna and Deidre?"

"They are doing great, except for missing their mamm and little bruder. We've been trying to keep them busy, so they don't miss you quite as much and they have been preoccupied playing with Mittens. They do love that little kitten. She came into their lives at a good time, ain't? She brings a lot of comfort to them and to all of us right now."

"I'll be so glad to get back home and see them again, as well as Ginger and Mittens. I just want everything to get back to normal again."

The three of us walked over to Matthew's bed and held hands as we made a circle around him. We took turns praying and after their hugs, they turned to leave.

That's when it happened...

CHAPTER 4

THE SUN HAD begun to set in the sky and shades of gold and purple began to bounce around the room with the reflection of the sunset. I walked over to the window and basked in its beauty as I was slowly combing my wet hair willing it to dry so I could put it back into its loose braid for bedtime.

After the sun finished its beautiful light show, I thanked the Lord for the beauty he had given us even in the midst of our sorrow. On my way back to my chair, I stopped by Matthew and touched his feverish brow and sang him another lullaby. Again he seemed to respond to my touch and voice as he did before. Again, I had hope that he would soon get better.

After finishing with my hair and brushing my teeth, I curled up in the recliner again to read the Bible. How I wished I had my own Bible with all my favorite verses marked, the ones that were such a comfort to me, but I would have to settle for the one that was left there on the stand.

I opened the word to Psalms. It has always been my go to book for comfort and wisdom. I read in Psalms 107:19-21: *"Then they cry unto the Lord in their trouble, and he saveth them out of their distresses. He sent his word, and healed them, and delivered them from their destructions. Oh that men would praise the Lord for his goodness, and for his wonderful works to the children of men!"*

What a promise. I couldn't help but wonder at the words. Was God telling me that little Mattie would be saved? How I longed for it to be so. I turned out the light and with a prayer still on my lips, I fell into a deep sleep with those words of God penetrating my heart.

"Samantha, wake up." I heard someone say through the fog of my sleep. I turned over and ignored the voice. "Samantha, wake up." Surely it was just a dream. Then the voice came back a third time. "Samantha Hoffman, wake up."

When the voice called me by my full name, it startled me. Someone was trying to get my attention. I woke up and looked around but there was no one in the room. I went to the nurses' station and asked if someone had called to me.

"No ma'am, we've been here since the beginning of the shift. Is there anything wrong? Is there a change in your baby?"

"Not that I'm aware of. I just heard someone calling my name, is all."

"You must have been dreaming," the nurse said.

I padded softly back to the room, and sat back down and prayed. I began dozing again, and as I did, I heard my name being called again. "Samantha, wake up."

"Who are you?" I said softly, "What do you want with me?"

As I became more awake, I noticed a soft glow in the room. It was brighter surrounding the crib. I immediately began to wonder if something was wrong with the monitors. Were their signals glowing more brightly for some reason? Was someone warning me that my baby was in danger?

I slowly walked over to the crib and everything seemed to be as it was before, but still the strange glow surrounded us. I had a warm comforting sensation like I was being hugged and comforted.

Then all of a sudden I heard loud alarms coming from all around me.

The nurses came rushing into the room screaming at me. "Mrs. Hoffman, what are you doing? Why did you take your baby out of the crib! You have disconnected all his monitors!" She took him from my arms and laid him back in the crib and replaced all of the leads to his chest and head. I was horrified as I realized that not only did his brain-wave and heart monitors become disconnected, but also the ventilator tubing came out.

The nurses called in the doctor that was on call, to let him know what happened. He rushed in immediately and was surprised to find that Mattie was breathing on his own and his oxygen readings were within normal limits without the ventilator.

"I'm going to leave the tube in until the morning, but we'll leave him off the ventilator. If he wakes up and starts fighting the tube, go ahead and remove it, but otherwise he can breathe with it while it is still inserted. If his oxygen levels are still okay, I'll take it out tomorrow."

The next morning when I awoke, I was completely disoriented. I forgot that I was in a hospital room until I looked over at the crib where my baby lay. He was still unresponsive and appeared to have everything still attached including the ventilator.

I began to panic. Had something gone wrong? Why did they reattach the ventilator? Could he still not breathe on his own?

I rang for the nurse and she came running into the room.

"What's wrong? Are you and Matthew all right?"

"Why is Mattie back on the ventilator?"

"What are you talking about?"

"During the night, the tubing got disconnected accidently when I picked him up and the doctor was going to leave it off until today if he continued to breathe on his own."

"Mrs. Hoffman, nothing happened during the night. Every time we came into the room to check on him, you were sound asleep. You were probably dreaming."

"You mean, I never picked him up and messed up all his monitors and I never came out when I kept hearing my name being called?"

"Nope, like I said, you've been asleep the whole time."

Strange, it felt so real! I picked up the Bible that was still lying open. It was opened to the verse I read last night in Psalms. I had a funny feeling in the pit of my stomach. Could a heavenly angel have visited me during the night? Was God sending me a message that my son was going to be okay? I prayed that it was so.

When I got up to go into the restroom to get ready for the day I was feeling a little lightheaded. I felt a little feverish so I asked the nurse if she would take my temperature. It was just slightly above normal, nothing to be concerned about, she had said. I splashed some cold water on my face, to wake up. When I went back into the room, she had brought in my breakfast tray. The smell of the eggs and bacon overwhelmed me and I grew nauseous. I turned around and headed back into the bathroom and vomited.

'Great,' I thought. *'All I need is to get a stomach bug now. I won't be any good to my son, if I have to keep away from him. That's the problem with hanging out in the hospital, you get all kinds of bugs.'*

The nurse came back into the room. "I heard you throwing up, are you okay?"

"Not right now, can you take this breakfast tray out? The smell is making me sick."

"You're not pregnant are you?"

"Not that I'm aware of. It is probably just a stomach bug."

"How about I bring you some crackers and ginger ale? That will help calm down your stomach some."

"Denki. I'd appreciate that."

Maybe I did just have a bad dream during the night. A stomach bug could have caused the dream, right?

The doctor came in after breakfast. He immediately started to examine Matthew.

"His color looks a little better today and his measles rash has started to fade. It looks like all his vital signs have begun to stabilize." Then he tested his eyes for pupil reaction and checked his reflexes. "His reflexes and pupils are showing a little reaction. The brain waves are increasing in strength. This little fella may just be trying to wake up."

"Such wunderbaar, gut news, doctor! I had a very vivid dream last night that angels were all around him and I held him and his ventilator became disconnected and you decided to leave it off him because he was trying to breath on his own."

"Well, I'm glad the part about the ventilator didn't happen, but I have no doubt that God and his angels are watching over him."

"Me too."

"I'm going to leave him on the ventilator for a little while longer, but this evening when I see him again, if he continues to show improvement, I may disconnect it temporarily to see if he starts breathing on his own. In the meantime, if you notice any changes, good or bad, let the nurse know and she'll contact me immediately."

He noticed me holding my stomach and trying to keep from being sick and passing out. "Are you alright?"

"Just a little light headed and sick on my stomach. All the excitement, I guess."

"You're not pregnant, are you?"

"I don't think so, it's probably something I ate, you know what this hospital food is like," I smiled.

"You take it easy, and let me know if you get worse. If it is a stomach bug, you probably shouldn't be around your son, and if you are pregnant, you have even more reason to stay away from him. Being exposed to someone with measles while your pregnant can be dangerous to the baby. Although, since you have been caring for him from the beginning of his illness, it's a little late to give you warnings about that."

"But, I've had all my vaccinations from my youth up, I should be immune to it. Wouldn't I have gotten sick by now if I was in any danger of contracting the disease?"

"You would have starting showing symptoms by now I would think. You might want to start a journal about how you're feeling, especially your physical symptoms. If your nausea gets better later in the day and returns again in the morning, I would highly recommend you taking a pregnancy test."

After the doctor left, I walked around in the room a bit, to see if I could get my stability back. I was still feeling somewhat lightheaded. I walked over to Mattie's crib and put my hand on his forehead. He felt much cooler this morning, hardly feverish at all. Except for the faded rash on his skin and all the tubes and monitor leads attached to his head and chest, he looked like a normal healthy baby, peacefully sleeping.

Tears came to my eyes, as I stared at him, wondering what our future held. I prayed that he would return to us as healthy as ever. As for the possibility of another child…I just couldn't think about that right now, I had enough on my plate with worrying about Mattie. He was my only concern at the moment. God would take care of the rest.

I didn't hear from my husband or my in-laws all morning, but I really didn't expect to. Mornings on the farm were especially hectic as they tried to get the animals fed and the cows milked and the crops seen to before the heat of the day. It was summer now and even in Lancaster County, the temperatures could get up in the nineties at times.

I was so thankful that my family believed in electricity, unlike some of my Old Order Amish friends in the area. I didn't know how they coped without air conditioning and electric fans.

I thought about the summer I was with Grandy Dee. For a couple of days following the small tornado that hit the area, we had to do without electricity. It wasn't too bad as long as the air was cool outside, but in the heat of the day, especially in the afternoons, it became unbearable. Of course, nothing was as bad as the day I fell asleep in the attic and suffered a slight heat stroke.

After we were married and following the death of my great grand-mother, we were blessed in that we were able to buy the house where I spent the summer with her. All of the old memories of that wonderful summer with her and my courtship with Ben were still floating around in that old house including the incident with the overheated attic and my heat stroke. I still have a hard time even thinking about going up there, even today, and I absolutely forbid my children to play up there in the summer, although sometimes they like to play in the attic during the winter.

Once when the weather was cooler, the girls were playing in the attic, I began to panic. They had become very quiet and visions of my passing out while I up there came to mind. I hurried to them, forget-ting my own fear and saw them going through some of their great aunt Jessica's old Bohemian hippy clothing and trying them on, giggling the whole time.

"Look at us, Mamma! We're beautiful!" Deidre smiled.

I had to smile at them, because I had once thought about trying them on myself. But instead of encouraging them to experiment with the look, I had to put my foot down. That wasn't the type of clothes that good little conservative Mennonite girls should be interested in.

Tears came to my eyes as I thought about my sweet girls. I missed them so much. Between being separated from them while I was at home, and now in the hospital with Matthew, it had been over a week since I had last seen them. I was ever so grateful that their dat and grandparents took such good care of them, but I couldn't wait to see them again.

I sat back down in my chair and decided to try and eat my crack-ers and drink my ginger ale and read the magazines that the nurse was kind enough to bring me. I found the article about my sister-in-law and her tearoom. It had some nice pictures of her and her family and of the newly renovated tearoom. It looked beautiful. It was in an old Victorian house that needed a lot of repairs, especially after a fire nearly destroyed it a few years before. Now, it was better than ever, but somehow she still managed to keep the same Victorian charm. The article went on to state how prosperous it had become, and how they gave God the glory for their success. What a blessing it was for her to praise God in a national magazine like that. What a blessing for all those who know her and frequent her tearoom. If I ever opened one, that would be how I would want people to think of me, that is, if I ever have the chance to open one.

While I was reading the article, the nurse walked in. "Mrs. Hoffman, there are two gentlemen out here wanting to visit you and Matthew, are you up for company?"

I peaked over her shoulder and saw Mr. Yoder, the preacher, and one of the deacons along with him.

"Sure, no problem," I smiled.

"Denki," he said, as he grinned at the nurse, and donned the protective gear. He walked over to me and took my hand. "How are you, Sister Samantha, and how is your wee boppli?"

"I'm coping, denki to Gott, and Mattie is stable right now. He's still in a coma, but the doctor expects him to wake up soon."

"That is wunderbaar, gut news! You know the church family is praying for your whole family. We've been missing you at service."

"I've missed being there. I've been keeping up with my scripture readings, and of course, I've been praying continually. Has Ben and the girls been coming to service?"

"Yes, Sister Linda and Brother John have made sure of that."

"Gut, I wouldn't want them to miss because of us. It's more important than ever to stay close to Gott now."

"Do you mind if we pray for you and your little one?" Pastor Yoder asked.

"Please do, I covet all the prayers of those who are willing to give them."

He and the deacon took my hands as we made a prayer circle. "Dear Heavenly Father, I pray that you will be with us, even as we stand here lifting up your name. Be with Sister Samantha and her son and give them comfort and healing. Bless them during this time of separation from her family. I pray for little Matthew that you will heal him completely with no residual problems from his illness, if it is your will, and be with your daughter and her family as they struggle to find peace in this situation. Thank you for bringing them this far. In Jesus precious and holy name, amen."

After they left, I settled back down with my snack. I was feeling somewhat better now and thought that maybe I'd be able to try some lunch when it came.

Not expecting anyone else to show up, I decided to take a walk down to the library and waiting room for a change of scenery. I was getting a little claustrophobic in the small room that had been my 'home' for the last two days. I stopped by the nurses' station to let them know I would be out of the room for a little bit.

The waiting room was light and pleasant. Along one wall were rows of books and magazines and there were also several tables and chairs for visitors to sit and wait for their loved ones or to get away from the sickness and death all around them.

While I was looking at the books, a young Amish woman came up to me. "Gut morning," she said.

"Gut morning to you, as well."

"My name is Sarah, Sarah Beiler, and you are?"

"I'm Samantha Hoffman. Are you here with a family member?"

She started crying. "My husband, Ezekiel, was going to market in our buggy and was hit by a car in the intersection. He has a broken leg and hit his head. He is in surgery right now to get his leg set. The doctor is worried about his head wound, too."

"I'm so sorry to hear about that. I hope he'll be okay."

"The doctor thinks he'll be alright, but I'm worried about how he'll feel when he finds out his favorite horse had to be put down."

"So the horse was hurt in the wreck?"

"Yes, the horse was hit directly by the car. Two of his legs were broken as well as some ribs. There just wasn't anything we could do to save him. Look, I'm sorry for burdening you with all my problems. I didn't even ask what you are here for."

"My baby bu is in a coma. He has the measles and suffered from a severely high temperature that caused some brain damage."

"Oh no, is he going to be okay?"

"The doctor is hopeful. I'm staying here with him. I just had to take a break from the room for a little bit."

"I could use a good cup of tea, can you stay away a bit longer and come have a cup with me?" Sarah asked.

"I would like that very much. I'm a big tea drinker myself and I've missed it since I've been here. They don't offer it on the meal trays."

"You should ask for it. I'll bet the nurses would get you some if you requested it. They may even have some at the nurses' station."

"I didn't think about that, denki."

We got to know each other better over our tea and Danishes. I found out that Sarah and her family lived a couple of miles from our farm. She and her husband shared the land with his dat and mamm and they had a set of twin girls. Like my girls, they were staying with their grandparents while we were here. At twenty-three, she was three years younger than I was and her husband was the same age as Ben.

We shared our addresses and other information with one another and I could see us becoming gut friends, a bond formed that day from the adversity of our circumstances. Until our loved ones left the hospital, I hoped to share more afternoon teas with her in the cafeteria. We even set up a time to meet the next day.

When I got back to my room I was surprised to see the doctor and two of the nurses standing over Mattie. I threw on my protective gown and gloves and rushed in the room.

"What is going on? Is Mattie okay? What's happening?" I cried out.

"Where have you been? We've been trying to find you!" The nurse said.

"I went to the day room and then to the cafeteria. Why did you need me?"

"The doctor has been waiting on you. He needed to get your permission to disconnect the ventilator to see if your son could breathe on his own. When you weren't here, we called your husband. He was very upset that you were gone from the room. He's on his way here."

"I told the nurses where I was going."

"You told the dayshift nurses, they evidently didn't pass the information on to us. Remember that next time, okay?"

I broke out in tears at the verbal tongue-lashing they gave me and I was afraid that Ben would be angry with me when he got here. I was so emotional today, I really had to wonder if my hormones were out of whack and the doctor was right about the possibility of my being pregnant. Of course, it could also just be the stress of the last few days. That made the most sense.

When the nurse saw me in tears, she apologized for being so sharp with me.

"I shouldn't have stayed so long away from the room. I'm sorry."

The doctor interrupted our conversation. "If it's alright with you two, can we get on with this now? I don't have all evening to spend with one patient."

They handed me the consent form to sign and the doctor disconnected the tube from his endotracheal tube to the ventilator. He wanted to sit and watch him and monitor his oxygen levels over the next few minutes. He would be right there in case Mattie got in trouble and he could reconnect the ventilator immediately, if it was needed.

As I watched him, I prayed that he would take a spontaneous breath and start breathing on his own and then start moving and responding to us, but I knew it was only wishful thinking on my part.

I was looking so intently at Mattie and the doctor, I didn't notice that Ben had walked through the door, until he walked up behind me and put his arms around my waist. I was grateful for his strength and support. Without it, I don't think I could have borne this trial we were going through. I leaned into his chest while still staring at our son.

The moment of truth was here.

CHAPTER 5

THE AIR IN the room was so tense you could slice it with a knife. The only sounds you could hear were the monitors recording every beat of his heart and the ventilator as it pushed the air into his lungs with its artificial breaths.

The moment of truth was on us. The doctor gradually decreased the number of respirations until the machine was turned completely off. Then he disconnected the tube. Mattie was starting to turn a sickly shade of blue as his pulse oximeter began to drop. It had gone from ninety nine to ninety to eighty-five. The doctor said if it dropped below eighty he would put him back on the breathing apparatus. I think I was holding my breath while I was willing my son to breathe on his own, as if by my not breathing, it would help him to start.

I kept watching the pulse oximeter, and the numbers slowly started creeping back up. I didn't want to look at my little boy, afraid that if I took my eyes off the monitor that it would quit rising. I prayed harder than I had ever done in my life. After it rose above ninety again, I looked at him and he was starting to turn pink again. I could see his little chest rising and falling in perfect rhythm.

"Well now, it looks like all your prayers have been answered, folks. I'm cautiously satisfied that he will be okay without the tube, so I'm going to go ahead and remove it. Mind you, he will have to be watched very closely over the next several hours to make sure he doesn't go into respiratory distress. I'm counting on you, Mr. and Mrs. Hoffman, to keep your eyes on him and let the nurse know if there are any changes. I'm still going to keep him on the heart and brain wave monitors and on his feeding tube until he wakes up. We will also keep an eye on his oxygen levels. We should know something for certain about his ability to maintain his breathing pattern by the time you go to sleep for the night. If he were to get in any distress the monitor alarms will wake you up. Do you have any questions?"

"Nothing I can think of right now," I said.

"The nurses will check on him pretty frequently over the next twenty-four hours, as well."

After the doctor and nurses left, Ben held me in his arms while we watched Mattie. His stomach slowly raised and fell as he continued to breath normally, none the worse for wear for what he had just gone through. I had hoped that the trauma of them pulling the tube out of his throat would wake him up, but he continued to lay there as lifeless as ever.

"So where were you today when the doctor was looking for you? I was worried about you when they called and said you weren't in the room."

"I'm sorry, Ben, but I had to get away for a little while. The walls of this room were closing in on me, and I wasn't feeling well this morning, probably because of the stress. I just needed a change of scenery and some fresh air."

"I can understand that, I'd be nuts going through what your doing right now. At least on the farm I can stay busy and get my mind off of things for a little while. I don't blame you at all. Just make sure the nurses know your exact location when you leave."

"Denki for being so understanding, I worried that you would be angry with me."

"Neh, not at all. We are going through enough problems without adding anger to the mix."

"Ben, I met a really nice Amish woman while I was out. That's why I was gone a little longer than I intended. She was here with her husband. He was in a traffic accident and had suffered a broken leg. He was in surgery when I met her. It seems a car had run into his horse and buggy. It turned the buggy over and he was injured. His horse ended up having to be put down because he was hurt too bad."

"Did they get the other driver?"

"I'm not sure, she didn't say. Her husband's name is Ezekiel Beiler and her name is Sarah. They live just a couple of miles from us."

"Zeke Beiler? We are friends from a while back. We grew up together. Our mothers attended some of the same work frolics and our fathers helped each other with harvesting."

"What a coincidence. Do you think we could we have them over to the house sometime? It would be ever so nice to have a friend close to my age, especially someone as nice as Sarah."

"Sure, I'd like to see old Zeke again too. Maybe when I come again tomorrow to visit, if Matthew is doing okay, we can go see them right quick."

"I was hoping to meet with her for some tea again tomorrow, but after all the grief they gave me today, I don't know if I'll be able to leave our room."

"We'll take one day at a time, my dear Samantha. The Lord takes care of the minutes and hours, one at a time. If he wills it, it will work out."

The nurse brought in my supper tray and gave us a little extra, so I could share it with Ben. My stomach was still a little unsettled, so I didn't eat much of my portion. Ben noticed.

"Sam, are you feeling ill?"

"I've had a little nausea today, it was worse this morning. After the nurse gave me some crackers and ginger ale, and I drank some chamomile tea this afternoon with my friend, it helped some, but I'm afraid after the excitement of this afternoon, I'm a bit queasy again."

"Do you want me to stay and help you? I'm sure my mamm and dat would be okay with keeping the girls overnight."

"Neh, you have your work you have to do, the animals will have to be tended to in the morning and besides, the girls need one of us to stay with them. I'll be all right. I'm sure it's just my nerves or a light stomach bug."

After my husband left and the nurse checked on Mattie and me and removed the tray from our room, I made a quick trip into the bathroom to wash my face and change from my long dress into to my nightgown. I removed my kapp from my hair and let down the bun that was pinned securely at the base of my neck. I was always amazed at how long my hair had gotten over the years since I joined the church. They frowned on women cutting their hair. They said it was a woman's glory, so I never cut it.

I walked back into the room and looked at my son before settling into my chair to brush my hair and braid it for the night.

It was so nice to see Mattie without the tube hanging out of his mouth, connected to a machine that was breathing for him. I prayed a prayer of thanksgiving that he was breathing on his own now. Hopefully, it was a good sign that he would wake up soon.

I thought about what Sarah had said earlier about asking the nurses if they had any tea on the unit, so I took a chance. I stepped into the hallway and called the nurse over.

"Would you happen to have some chamomile tea? My stomach is still a little upset, and maybe it would help me rest a little better."

"I think we have some. She went to the back and came back with a Styrofoam cup filled with hot water and a teabag and some sugar and creamer on the side."

"Thank you so much, and I want to apologize for earlier for not being here when you needed me," I said.

"No problem, I shouldn't have fussed at you, I can certainly understand your need to get away for a few minutes. Enjoy your tea and if you need anything else at all, please let me know."

"Thank you for being so kind."

She decided to check on Matthew while she was at the room. "Do you want me to give him his bath now?"

"Can I do it tonight, I miss bathing my little boy."

"Sure, if that's what you want. I'll bring his basin of water and soap in a few minutes. In the meantime, I'll give you a little while to drink your tea in peace."

I continued to read my Bible while I enjoyed my tea. The verse I read tonight was Psalms 116:1-7: *I love the Lord because he hath heard my voice and my supplications. Because he hath inclined his ear unto me, therefore will I call upon him as long as I live. The sorrows of death compassed me, and the pains of hell got hold upon me: I found trouble and sorrow. Then called I upon the name of the Lord; O Lord, I beseech thee, deliver my soul. Gracious is the Lord, and righteous; yea, our God is merciful. The Lord preserveth the simple: I was brought low, and he helped me. Return unto thy rest, O my soul; for the Lord hath dealt bountifully with thee.*

I closed my Bible and said a quick prayer. The passage was a soothing balm to my soul. I knew the Lord was in control and no matter what happened over the next few days, I would trust him to take care of it. Even if he called my sweet boy home to himself, I believed that I could even accept that.

The nurse came into the room with the bathing supplies and a fresh diaper; the only piece of clothing my son wore since he'd been here.

"Be careful as you wash him, to not disturb the monitor leads still attached to him. Wash around them as carefully as possible. You'll be tempted to wash his hair, but don't. It's okay to turn him from side to side, to wash his back, but just be careful. Also wear a gown and gloves whenever you touch him. Although his rash seems to be clearing up there may still be a raw and draining scab that is somewhere on his body. Understand?"

"Yes ma'am. I'll be very careful."

"We use a special soap that won't dry out his skin, and we have a cream to put on his rash. Just put it on him after you dry him off. Let me know if there are any new lesions or ones that you're concerned about, okay?"

"Thank you, I will."

I enjoyed bathing my little boy again and lovingly touched every inch of his body that was free of the electrical monitor leads. His measles rash seemed more faint now and I was happy about that. He looked like he felt miserable a few days earlier when he was awake. He just couldn't get comfortable. I guess it was a blessing in disguise that he was in a coma the last few days while his skin was healing. After I washed his back and covered it with the cream, I put his diaper on, and started to put the cream on his legs and arms.

As I made my way down his little arm into his hand, I thought I felt something. Was he trying to grip my finger? I repeated the sequence on the other side with his other arm and the same thing happened.

I called the nurse in and told her what he had done.

"Don't get too excited, Mrs. Hoffman. It could be an involuntary reflex, but still it gives me hope. Even involuntary reflexes signify that there is brain activity. Let me know if you see any other changes."

I wasn't ready to leave my child's side after bathing him, so I brought a chair over next to the crib and sat holding his little hand. I turned him on his side so he could get off his back for a little bit.

As I sat there, I felt at peace. I laid my head down next to him and fell asleep. Later, I woke up when a soft light entered the room that had been darkened for the night. I was still next to him and the light startled me. I figured it was the nurse coming in to check on him, but when I looked around, no one was there.

I heard a voice. Not an audible one, but one coming from my deep inside me. *'Samantha, your prayers have been heard,'* it seemed to say.

I looked at Mattie, and he was lying on his back again and no longer had a hold on my finger. He still looked like he was sleeping peacefully and his breathing was stable, so I went back to my chair and fell asleep.

I woke up a few minutes later to see the nurse come in with her flashlight to check on him. No sooner had she left the room, than I heard a soft rustling sound coming from the crib. I turned on the night-light next to my chair and padded over to him. Was this another dream? Was I hallucinating? Mattie was trying to turn over and sit up! I called for the nurse.

"What's going on it here?" she asked as she entered the room.

"Look at Matthew! He's trying to sit up!"

She hurried over to his crib. He was lying as still as ever.

"Mrs. Hoffman, I don't see any changes in him. You must be seeing things again."

"I swear to you, I saw him! He turned on his side and then came up to a sitting position!"

"Well, he's not doing it now, he looks the same as ever. Try to get some sleep. Things will be more clear in the morning, just like yesterday."

"I guess I'd better. Thank you for checking on us."

The next morning I woke up and my nausea had returned with a vengeance. Something was definitely wrong.

The nurse came in and found me vomiting in the bathroom. "Mrs. Hoffman, are you alright?"

"I don't know what's happening. I was sick yesterday and now again today."

"Let me get you some crackers and tea, will that help?"

"It might. Denki."

I brushed my teeth and rinsed my mouth out and quickly changed into my dress and put my hair back up into a bun. Just as I finished, the doctor came in.

"Mrs. Hoffman, we need to find out what's going on with you. I would like to do a pregnancy test on you to rule that out, if that's alright with you."

"That's for the best, I guess. I'm not sure that's what it is, but I'll do whatever you say."

"If you are pregnant, I want you to see a doctor as soon as you get out of here. You'll need to be followed closely since you've been exposed to the measles. Of course, if it's negative, it will be one less thing for you to worry about, and we'll see what else could be causing your symptoms. It's a possibility that it is nothing but nerves."

"Did the nurse tell you what happened during the night?"

"She said that you called her in the room because you thought you saw Matthew trying to sit up, but when she came in he was still out of it."

"Am I going crazy and seeing things?" I asked.

"I don't think you are crazy, but our brains like to play tricks on us. Call it wishful thinking. You want him to be well and so you imagine him so. There's nothing wrong with that. I'd probably be the same way, if he were my child."

"But the night before last, I saw him getting his breathing tube out and yesterday you took it out."

"Most likely a coincidence or maybe you're a prophet," he grinned. "Do Mennonites believe in modern day prophets, Mrs. Hoffman?

"I don't think so, not like that, anyways. I would never compare myself to someone with the gift of prophecy."

The doctor left just as the nurse brought in my breakfast tray. I still wasn't very hungry and I asked her to take it away except for the cereal and milk. I would try to see if I could keep that down.

A little while later the nurse came back with a pregnancy test. "The doctor ordered this for you, Samantha. He wants you to go ahead and test yourself today to see if that's what is causing your nausea."

"I really don't think I am, but I guess it can't hurt."

I was nervous about the test. What if I were pregnant? How would Ben react to the news? Mattie just turned a year old, could I handle another wee one so soon after Matthew? That is, if Mattie survived this illness.

I couldn't put it off any longer. After eating my breakfast, I took the test kit into the bathroom with me.

CHAPTER 6

THE DOCTOR'S SUSPICIONS were right. The pregnancy test confirmed it. I worried about how Ben was going to react when he found out. At least now I knew why I felt light headed and sick on my stomach and how come I was so emotional lately.

I let the nurse know the results, but I begged her to let me tell Ben myself.

I had the urge to call him, but I wanted to tell him in person, so I could tell what his real reaction was.

Mixed with the happiness, I had my fears as well. The doctor warned me about what could happen to the baby with me being exposed to the measles. There was a danger of birth defects, premature birth and even miscarriage. None of those things was something I wanted for our baby. Now along with praying for my sweet little Matthew, I would also have to include his little brother or sister.

Everything became overwhelming once I got the news. Again my emotions got the better of me and the world started spinning out of control again. I curled up in my chair in the corner and buried my head and wept.

After a few minutes, I felt a nudge on my shoulder. "Mrs. Hoffman," I continued to bury my head. "Samantha," she said again.

At first I didn't look, thinking it was my imagination, but after tapping my shoulder again I turned and saw the nurse standing over me.

"Come here, I have something to show you," she said, smiling.

I followed her over to the crib where Matthew was laying.

"His eyes are open!" I cried. I took his little hand in mine and he squeezed my finger. He looked at me and then at the nurse.

"Mamma," was all he said, but for me it was enough. My baby was awake and he knew who I was. I asked the nurse if I could pick him up and hold him, and she said I could as long as I was careful with his monitor leads and his feeding tube.

It was so good to hold him in my arms again. It had been well over a week now since I last held him in his room at home, trying to comfort him and bring down his raging fever. This time he snuggled against me like he never wanted to let go. His temperature had at last returned to normal.

I sat in the chair and was holding him, when the doctor came into the room.

"Well young lady, it seems your vision during the night came true again," he smiled. "Would you like to try to feed him again? I'd like to take his feeding tube out and see if he'll eat normally. Also since he appears to be wide awake, I'm going to take his monitor leads off, then you can give him a proper bath and wash the glue out of his hair."

"I'm not going to be able to nurse him, am I? I think my breast milk is probably dried up by now."

"Unfortunately, you will need to feed him by bottle until he's weaned. We'll give you the formula that he had in his tube feeding and then we'll gradually transition him over to regular milk. I know it won't be the same for you but it will be a reasonable alternative. Besides, since you are pregnant, your body will have to prepare itself for the new little one. Speaking of which, I would like to talk with you and your husband this afternoon after he has learned of your condition. Congratulations on all of your good news today. I'm so happy that your son is back with us and appears to have no residual problems. I do plan on keeping him in the hospital for one more day to make sure he doesn't have any setbacks, but if he continues to improve, I don't see any reason why he can't go home tomorrow."

It was amazing how much better I felt. The joy of being able to hold Mattie, and knowing I was pregnant with another wee one did much to improve my illness earlier in the day.

The nurse brought in his washbasin, soap, shampoo, and lotion, along with a washcloth and towel. She even brought in a small pair of hospital pajamas to put him in. It was nice to be able to wash his hair and his whole body. His rash was almost entirely gone now and he was no longer contagious. We could hold him without having to wear all of the protective gear now and it was wonderful.

After I bathed him, I sat in the rocking chair in the room, holding him, and I tried to feed him a bottle of milk, but he didn't seem to get the idea of feeding with it. I expressed my concern to the nurse, but she said he might still be full from the tube feeding and try again a little later. If he still had problems, even when he was hungry, than dip my finger in the formula and let him suck on it and then gently replace my finger with the nipple. I tried it and he quickly picked up on what I was trying to do and he was fine after that.

Ben was sure pleasantly surprised when he arrived that afternoon.

I was still rocking Mattie and he came in and threw his arms around both of us.

"I don't believe it! Why didn't you call me?" he asked

"What, and miss the surprise on your face?"

"You look like you're feeling better, too. I guess the stress you've been feeling, is better now."

"I am feeling better about Matthew, that's for certain, but while I have you in such a good mood, there is something else I need to tell you about. I think you'd better sit down."

He sat and eyed me suspiciously. He didn't know what was coming.

"You know that the last few days I've felt sick to my stomach and have been light headed."

"Yes, but I figured it was because of the stress you were under, or being cooped up here in the hospital and around other sick people."

"The doctor was concerned about me, and wanted to rule out some things. Well the first thing he wanted to test me for was if I was pregnant."

"And…?"

"It turns out, I am." I frowned. "Please don't be angry."

"Are you kidding me? I couldn't be happier! You know I want a large family," he smiled.

I stood and we hugged. The three of us together, then he took Matthew from my arms and gave him a big hug. "Welcome back to us son! You're going to be a big bruder! This day keeps getting better!"

I sat back down and Ben noticed the frown on my face.

"What's wrong, Sam?"

"Oh it is probably nothing, the doctor has some concerns about me being around Mattie while I'm pregnant. He's going to come and talk to us later about it."

"I didn't think about that. I pray that everything will be okay. Too bad we didn't know about it sooner. We'll just have to trust God that he will work everything out for us."

The doctor came in while we were playing with Mattie. "You two look happy," he said, smiling. "I hope after I get through talking to the two of you, I don't dampen your spirits too much."

"I hope not, doctor," Ben said.

"Well, let's start with the good news. Mr. Matthew is doing great and he looks wonderful. If he doesn't have any setbacks tonight, I see no reason why he can't go home tomorrow. Since his fever and rash are gone he should no longer be contagious and will be able to blend back in with your other children without any danger to them. But let this be a lesson to you. You've seen how dangerously ill he became from this disease. If you've not had your other children vaccinated, I would highly recommend it."

"Do you think he'll be okay now?"

"When he was admitted with a high fever, he had some seizures, as you know. There could be a possibility that he suffered some brain damage. Only time will tell if there are any lasting effects from it. I will want to follow up with him every few months to see if he is progressing at a normal rate."

"What about Samantha and the baby?" Ben asked.

"I was just getting to that. I have no way of knowing how far along that you are, Mrs. Hoffman, that will make some difference in the types of problems you could have from being exposed to the measles. The other factor is; since you had the measles vaccine and are immune to the disease, you may not have any problems at all with your pregnancy. The worse danger is to those who actually get the disease when they are pregnant, however, I want you to be checked out by a obstetrician as soon as possible and you're going to have watch your pregnancy closely."

"What are the dangers, doctor?" Ben asked.

"Worst case scenarios are; you could have a miscarriage or a premature baby, or the baby could be stillborn. If the child were to get the infection while you're carrying it, it could result in heart, liver, or brain problems."

"That sounds bad," I frowned.

"Well I do want to give you some hope, like I said you evidently are immune, so more than likely, nothing has been passed on to the fetus. Everything should be okay, and there's no reason to believe that you won't have anything other than a perfectly healthy baby, but as I said, I do want you to get seen as soon as possible by your OB doctor and let me be the first to congratulate both of you on the new little one and for

Mr. Matthew getting well. I'll be by first thing in the morning to check in on you and hopefully to get your discharge taken care of."

"Thank you, doctor," Ben smiled.

"I'll see you in the morning," I added as he turned to leave.

After he left, Ben took me in his arms and gave me a big hug and kiss. I was worried that the nurse would walk in on us, but she didn't.

"So Mrs. Hoffman, how are you feeling about everything that happened today?" Ben smiled.

"Excited, but concerned too. I'll feel better about everything as soon as we learn everything is okay."

"What about you, Mattie, my boy? You ready to be a big bruder?" he asked as he picked him up and poked him in the belly.

All Mattie said was "Dada" and started sucking his thumb.

"I think we should call our folks and let them know all of our good news. Won't the girls be excited for you to come back home with Matthew and start preparing for the baby?"

"I want to call my parents and give them the good news, too, but we'll have to wait until we get back to the house and use our phone."

I thought about my new friend, Sarah, I wanted to let her know what was happening and get her phone number and address so I could keep in touch with her.

"Ben, do you mind if I go to Sarah and Ezekiel's room to let her know we'll be leaving and give her the good news about Mattie?"

"Sure, just don't be gone too long. I'd like to drop by and see old Zeke myself to wish him well. While you're there, see if he'd mind a visit from me, too."

I got their room number from the nurses after they checked their computers.

When I got to their room, Sarah greeted me with a hug and introduced me to her husband. He looked well, but he had to be uncomfortable lying there with his leg up in a sling suspected from an overhead bar.

"I'm sorry I didn't get a chance to meet you for tea yesterday. There was some things going on with my baby and I had to stay in my room."

"Ach, neh! I hope he's okay!"

"Better than okay, they were taking him off the ventilator and they wanted me to be there. He's doing fine and we're going home tomorrow!"

"That's wunderbaar, gut news!"

"Yes, it is wonderful! I can't wait to get back home with the rest of my family, but I will miss getting a chance to see you again!"

"We can still be friends, ain't? We don't live that far away from each other," Sarah frowned.

"I was hoping you would say that, because it would be wonderful to have someone my age close by that I can visit with sometimes."

I looked at her husband. "Mr. Beiler, my husband, Ben, said that you and he grew up together."

"I believe, you're right, how is Ben doing?"

"He's doing well, he'd like to come by and visit you if it's all right with you. He's up in my son's hospital room right now."

"Sure I'd love to see him. Maybe the four of us and the kinner could visit after we're out of this place."

"I think my girls would love to meet yours. Is it all right if Ben stops by on his way home tonight?"

"I can't wait. Send him down, and by the way Mr. Beiler is my father, you can call me Zeke."

"Denki, I will. That's how Ben remembers you, too."

We exchanged addresses and phone numbers. Sarah said that they didn't have their own phone, but they shared a phone outside of their home with a couple of other families in their area. I promised her that if the Lord willed, we would get together again sometime after we were both back home.

That evening Ben left to go home and visited Zeke on his way out.

The next day as we were leaving, we stopped by their room to say goodbye, but their room was empty. The nurse said they were discharged earlier in the day.

On our way out of the hospital, we went by the financial office to arrange to pay our bill, but when we sat down with them, they checked our record to see what we still owed, and after checking her computer the woman said that our bill had been paid in full.

"How is that possible?" I asked. "We haven't paid anything on it."

"The person who paid it wanted to remain anonymous," she answered, smiling. "Congratulations on your baby getting well and please take care of yourselves. God bless your family."

"Thank you ma'am, he already has," Ben grinned at her. God bless you as well.

CHAPTER 7

WHEN WE ARRIVED back at the house, Ben's parents and the girls were already there.

As soon as the car pulled into the driveway, Deedee and Anna came running and squealing, as they were so excited to see their little bruder and me.

"Mamma, Mattie! Mamma's home!" Deedee grinned.

I handed Matthew over to his father, so I could give a proper hug to my sweet girls. I missed them so much! I've not been able to hold them or even get close to them in almost two weeks and we were long overdue for the closeness I longed for with them.

After hugging the girls, next came my in-laws. I was ever so blessed to have such a special relationship with them.

A wunderbaar smell was coming from the kitchen when I walked through the door. Mamma Linda had baked some fresh bread that morning and cooked a pot of chicken stew. I was ever so grateful that my morning sickness had passed for the day, and I was feeling famished by the time we arrived home at lunchtime.

The girls were very clingy because they missed me so much, and I had to say that I didn't mind it one bit. Ben didn't act too interested in returning to his chores either and lingered over some tea after lunch. I think he was enjoying seeing the interaction between us.

We decided that this would be a good time to tell the girls that there was going to be another little one in a few months.

"Just like Ginger!" laughed Anna.

"Mamma, are you going to give away the new baby?" Deedee asked, frowning.

"Heavens no, whatever gave you that idea?"

"Dat said that we had to give away Ginger's babies. He said we couldn't 'ford another mouth to feed."

"Well, we can't afford any more pets, but a new little bruder or sister isn't the same thing. They are part of the family just like you girls are."

"Can't we keep one of the puppies…please?" begged Anna.

"You'll have to talk to your dat about that. Besides you already have a new kitten to play with or did you forget? Where is she by the way?"

"She's in the kitchen with Mammi Hoffman. She's getting some chicken from her."

"Sounds like all of you have gotten her good and spoiled while I was out."

"Jah, we did, but she's so cute when she begs for food, you can't help but give in to her," Ben grinned.

"So she has you all wrapped around her finger, ain't."

"We may decide to keep one of the pups. Since the girls have taken over the kitten, Matthew and I need to have a guy pet," he laughed. "The girls can take care of it until Matthew grows a bit. That okay with you girls?"

"Denki, Dat!" squealed Deidre. "We can do that!"

"Remember, it will be Mattie's when he can take care of it," I reminded them.

"But it will be ours until then," they smiled as they walked off hand in hand.

I loved that our little girls were so close. Not only in age, but also in spirit. Without other children living close by, they had only each other to play with. There were a few children in our church, but everyone seemed to live miles away. I hoped that my friendship with Sarah Beiler would grow, because she would be a wunderbaar friend for me and Zeke, her husband, could be a buddy to Ben, and as a bonus she had a couple of girls close to our girls ages. How I truly longed to see her and her family again. It would be such a blessing for all of us.

After lunch I shooed the girls out to play while I unpacked my bag of dirty clothes from the hospital. I decided to go ahead and do a load of clothes and hang them on the clothesline, so the sun could bleach them out and sanitize them. Mamma Linda told me early on when Ben and I were talking marriage that there would be a lot of changes in the way I lived, and hanging out laundry was one of the things I had to learn to do, and ironing them after they were dried. I found that I loved the way the clean clothes smelled after being in the sun all day. Now I couldn't imagine ever using a dryer again.

I put Mattie in his walker and brought him out near the clothesline so I could keep my eyes on him while I was outside. He normally loved the walker and could even scoot around the yard some, even though the grass slowed him down a bit. Today he was unusually quiet and looked like he just wanted to sleep. I guess that wasn't too unusual because of what he had been through the last few days. I didn't keep him out too long this day, because I didn't want him getting overheated.

As soon as I finished the clothes, I took him back inside and put him to bed for a nap after changing and feeding him. Then it was time to gather some fresh vegetables from the garden for our supper. It felt good to be outside again and more or less back to normal.

There was still some leftover chicken stew from lunch, but I thought a nice fresh salad would be good with it. I also made some cookies for dessert; chocolate chip, my family's favorite. They would be so good with a bowl of vanilla ice cream, a special treat for our first day home.

I let the girls help me with the cookies, but it seems like they ate more of the dough than I put on the cookie sheet. Still, it was nice to be doing things with them again.

Ben was out in the barn cleaning out the horse stalls and doing some repair work to it's exterior. Seems like there was always something to do on a farm. It sure kept him busy.

I smiled as I saw Ginger following him everywhere. I so thankful, that she was all right after that scare with the broken glass. She was getting bigger in the abdomen now with her four pups beginning to take up so much space. This was her first, and hopefully, her last litter of pups. I could certainly sympathize with her after going through a pregnancy three times already and working on my fourth. We didn't know what to expect from her pups because we had no idea where the puppies' daddy came from.

The summer was particularly hot this year, especially for Lancaster County. It felt more like the ones I had lived through in the south in the past. I was so thankful that we were allowed to have electricity in our homes, unlike some of our Amish neighbors. I don't think I would have made it without air conditioning, especially now that I was pregnant and my hormones were so out of control.

I tried to find things to do inside the cool house, and left the outside farm chores to Ben. The girls liked to run around behind him and help where they could, but I kept Matthew inside with me. He just wasn't rebounding from his illness like I thought he should and he seemed to do worse with the heat. I only brought him outside when it was cooler in the mornings or evenings and when I needed to be outside with my laundry. After almost losing him, I couldn't bear letting him out of my sight.

Our garden did real well this year, so I kept busy canning and cooking. I canned preserves, green beans, corn, tomatoes, squash, tomato sauce, and applesauce and apple butter.

I made extra jars of preserves and apple butter to sell at the farmers' market, along with some crocheted doilies and pillows and some rag dolls for my younger customers. We had a booth at the market that met every weekend during the summer.

We all loved going to market, it was a great time to meet up with our neighbors and share stories with one another, that is, when we weren't waiting on customers.

There were a lot of Englischers who came to the market. They enjoyed all of the homemade Amish and Mennonite foods, quilts, furniture, and many other handmade things. I think the appeal to outsiders was that not only were they getting quality goods, and fresh fruit and vegetables, but also for the few minutes they were there, they would feel they were back in a quieter and more peaceful time. Also, I'm sure some of them were there out of curiosity about the Amish and Mennonites. I know if I were still an outsider that's how I would feel coming here. Of course, the tourists had no idea how much work went into the things they bought. Hours, days, and sometimes weeks went into making some of the things we were selling. Many of the cloth items we sold were stitched by hand and it was a very tedious job.

One Saturday, while we were sitting at our booth, I was looking down at Matthew, when I heard a familiar voice call out to me. "Samantha?"

I looked up and saw my friend, Sarah, from the hospital.

"Sarah! It's wunderbaar, gut to see you!" I smiled. "Are you here buying or selling?"

"A little bit of both, actually. I spotted your dolls you made. They are delightful! I'd like to get one for each of my girls. I want to surprise them."

"Where are your girls today?" I asked.

"They are playing with the other children in the play area."

"Really? Mine are over there, as well. They may actually be playing together. Wouldn't it be nice, if they became friends, too?"

"Jah that would be gut. It would make it nicer when we visit with one another someday," Sarah replied.

"Who is watching your sales stand?"

"Zeke is over there now, I believe your husband found him."

"What are you selling?"

"We have honey and homemade preserves. Zeke has made some rocking chairs and ladder-back chairs. He is a wunderbaar carpenter."

"I would love to get a couple of rocking chairs for our front porch, but with our new wee one coming in a few months, I'm afraid we don't have much money right now."

"Maybe, we could make a trade. I want your rag dolls, and you want our chairs."

"Let's talk to our husbands first. They may want to get the money as opposed to bartering. I don't have a problem with it, but it will be their decision."

"I understand, especially since we have doctor bills to be paid, as well." Sarah frowned.

"Oh my goodness. I almost forgot about Zeke's broken leg! How did he get here?"

"His fifteen year old bruder, Isaiah, is staying with us until Ezekiel can walk again. Ezekiel and our girls rode in the back of the wagon with our wares and I rode up front with him. He helped him get on and off the wagon."

"I'll bet he's a great help in a time like this."

"Jah, he is. Ezekiel is starting to get 'narrish', crazy, as you would say, having to sit around and not being able to do anything. So he gets out and hobbles on his crutches trying to do things. I'm worried that he's going to aggravate his injury by doing too much. He doesn't know how to stop if he starts hurting," Sarah frowned.

"I think Ben would be the same way if that happened to him."

"Well, I pray it never does. Menfolk are the worse patients ever."

About that time the girls came running up to us. "Mamma, we found some new friends!" Deidre said breathlessly.

Sarah's two girls came up behind them and ran to their mother.

"Samantha, this is Rebekah and Rachel, my maedels."

"Nice to meet you, girls. Sarah, these two are Deidre and Anna."

"Deidre is an unusual name for a Mennonite girl," she said.

"We named her after my great grandmother. Her name was Deidre. I called her my Grandy Dee. We nicknamed our daughter, Deedee. As a matter of fact, we bought my great grandmother's farm after she died. That's where we are living now."

"That's gut. I'm glad you are living here close by. I'm sorry about your grandmother passing, though."

"Me too, but she lived to be one hundred years old, and she's with Jesus now and with my great grandfather in heaven and I can't be sad about that."

As we were visiting, Ben came back to the table. He spoke to Sarah, "Zeke is looking for you and the girls. He wants to start packing up everything and head home. It looks like a storm is trying to move in and he wants to get home before it starts raining."

"Ben, Sarah is interested in getting a couple of the dolls I made for her girls and I was interested in getting one of their rockers for our front porch. If it's all right with Zeke and you, can we make a trade?"

"If Zeke's okay with it, I am."

So the trade was made. I let Rebekah and Rachel choose their favorite dolls and we picked out one of the rockers and loaded it on the truck along with the rest of our unsold goods and headed home.

No sooner had we arrived back at the house and stored all of our things away, then the heavens opened up and the rains came with a vengeance.

Ben ran out to the farmyard to get the animals into the barn when it began to thunder and lightning, and the hail started to fall soon after they were all inside. The winds began to pick up quickly and the first thing I thought of was the storm that hit our house the summer I spent with Grandy Dee. We had been hit by a small tornado and it had started out the same way as this storm.

Fearing the worst, and a repeat of that summer, I gathered the children, and an oil lantern, and headed into the fruit cellar.

It seemed like hours that we were huddled together in the dark damp basement, but I know it couldn't have been more than a few minutes. The girls were scared and even though Matthew was quiet, I could feel the tension in his body as I held him.

"I know, how would you girls like a story?" I asked, trying to lighten the tension.

"Jah, that would be gut!" exclaimed Deedee.

I started thinking about the fairy tales from when I was little. I'm not sure what the church would think about such secular tales, but my primary concern was getting my children relaxed in a scary situation. I thought about telling them about the three little pigs, but somehow a story about a house being blown down by a big bad wolf or some other means would be too scary right now, especially with the wind howling outside, so I told them the story of Goldilocks and the three bears.

Through the telling of the story and the loud winds and thunder overhead, the girls and I almost jumped out of our skins several times. I was amazed that little Matthew slept through the whole thing. How nice it must be that it didn't seem to even faze him.

I worried about Ben. I prayed that he had gotten safely back to the house, but I had to wonder why he didn't join us in the cellar. When I didn't hear any movement upstairs, I figured that he probably stayed in the barn with the animals and not risk trying to make his way back to the house in the wind and hail. That is probably what I would've done.

When the winds died down and the thunder and lightning stopped, the children and I made our way back upstairs. The power had gone out, probably because of the storm, but thankfully, it was still daylight and the house seemed to be intact.

Since Matthew was still asleep, I put him to bed in his crib and the girls and I went outside to survey the damage. There were tree branches everywhere, but at least they had fallen away from the house. I looked toward the barn expecting to see Ben out and checking on the animals and damage to the fences and outbuildings, but he was nowhere in sight. I kept calling out his name, but I didn't get a response.

I turned to the girls. "I want you two to go ahead and start picking up the sticks in the yard and piling them up in neat piles, can you do that for me?"

As they were picking up the sticks, I headed toward the barn. The first thing I noticed was that the fence gate and barn door were left open. Had he opened it up after the storm was over? I could understand the barn door, but he would have never left the gate open for animals to get out of the yard. I guess it could have blown open in the storm.

I entered the barnyard and called for him. "Ben, I closed the gate. Are you in here?"

There was no answer, so I quickly looked around to make sure that no animals were missing. The animals were still there, but there on the floor was something I didn't expect to see and I was terrified with what I saw.

CHAPTER 8

"BEN!" I SCREAMED so loudly that the girls came running. "Wake up!" I yelled louder.

I knelt over him and checked for a pulse, like I learned in CPR class in high school. I'm glad I never forgot what to do. I was thankful that I felt a pulse and saw that he was still breathing.

As I was checking him over, the girls came into the barn. When they saw their father lying on the floor of the barn they started crying. They ran over to him and tried to hug him.

"Dat, wake up, wake up!" they said one after the other.

We heard the sound of crunching gravel when a van pulled up in the driveway.

The girls ran out and saw their grandfather get out.

"Dawdy, Dawdy! Dat is hurt, please come!" they said as they pulled him to the barn.

By the time they came back inside, Ben had started to wake up. I checked him over to see what kind of injuries he had and that's when I saw a rather large bump on the back of his head.

I stayed with him while his dat went to the kitchen to bring back some ice and a damp towel to clean him off. The girls stayed with us until their father had awoken completely.

"Son, you had probably ought to go let the doc take a look at this injury. With you passed out like that, you more than likely had a concussion."

"Can you take him, John? I probably shouldn't leave the children. Matthew is down for a nap and I should stay here for him and the girls would only be underfoot at the clinic."

"That would probably be for the best, Sam. We'll let you know something as soon as we find out how he is."

"That is, if the telephones are working. Our electricity is off, but I haven't checked the phones."

"I didn't think about that, I came over to check on you because I couldn't get through by phone. Hopefully, they'll be back on soon," John frowned.

"He needs to get to the doctor right away, you can contact me when you can, in the meantime, hopefully, you may be back home with Ben at your side."

After John left with Ben, I looked around the barn to see what could have hurt him like that. I figured that a tree limb or large hailstone hit him in the head and he staggered into the barn and fell.

It was then, I almost tripped over a shovel that was lying in the middle of the floor not too far from where Ben was laying.

'It's not like Ben laying things around like that.' I thought. Then I picked it up I saw a pair of gloves lying nearby. *'Ben must have been really out of it to throw that shovel and gloves in the middle of the floor.'*

I picked up the shovel to hang it back on the wall and I gasped when I saw the blood on it. This wasn't an accident. It looked like someone may have intentionally hit him in the head!

If someone was out to hurt him, or us, for some reason, they could still be in the area. I grabbed the girls and ran back to the house and locked the doors.

"Mamma, what's going on?" Anna cried.

I didn't answer her but ran from room to room making sure everyone was safe and there was no one hiding in the house. I locked all the windows after checking everywhere.

"Deedee and Anna, I need you to go and stay in your room and play until your dat and dawdy John gets back, understand?"

"But why? Did we do something wrong?" Deedee looked at me with tears in her eyes.

"No, honey girl, you and your sister have been perfect. I just need to be careful right now while your dat is gone. I'll explain everything after he comes back home. You've been so brave through the storm and seeing your dat hurt. I just need you to be brave a little bit longer. Can you do that?"

"Yes, Mamma," frowned Deidre, and her sister Anna echoed her.

I tried calling out and the phone lines were still down, as was the electricity. I hated to have the windows closed and latched, making the house even hotter, but I couldn't take any chances right now. I just prayed we would get the electricity back on soon, so we could cool down the house.

Through all the excitement, I almost forgot about Matthew. I ran to his room to make sure he was okay. When I saw him, he was sitting up, quietly playing with his toys in the crib.

"Mattie! Sorry to ignore you for so long, Mamma's been too busy." He didn't turn to look at me and kept on playing with his toys.

I leaned over to pick him up to change him. "Mamma," he smiled when he saw me.

I changed his diaper and put it in the bathroom to soak until I could wash it and then went to the kitchen to prepare a bottle of formula for him for his supper. I so wish, I could nurse him like before he got sick, but that changed while he was in the hospital and so ill that had to take formula through his nasogastric tube. After that he would no longer take my breast milk.

While the girls were in their room playing with the dollhouse that Grandy Dee left me, and now belonged to my girls, I rocked Mattie and fed him in his room.

After I'd been sitting and holding him for a few minutes, I heard a knock on the door. Had John and Ben returned? I quickly put Mattie back in his crib and ran downstairs hoping to see that my husband had come home.

When I got to the door, a policeman met me outside on the porch. "Mrs. Hoffman?"

"Yes sir, that's me. What can I do for you?" I asked nervously, worried that something had happened to dawdy John and Ben.

"We're looking for an escaped prisoner and we're checking all the local farms. We decided to come by here first, because of the connection you have with the prisoner."

"What? We don't know anyone like that."

"Have you forgotten so soon? Six or seven years ago your husband was kidnapped, beaten, and left for dead. The man who did that is the one who has escaped."

"Oh no! Officer, something has happened that I think you need to see."

I took him out to the barn and showed him the shovel and gloves.

"I found my husband unconscious here on the floor and this shovel was close by. He had a head wound, but I figured he was injured in the storm and came in the barn and fell and threw the shovel down. When I picked up the shovel I saw the blood on it and then I saw the gloves close to it."

"I wish you hadn't picked the shovel up, but you couldn't have known that this was a potential crime scene. Where is your husband now?"

"My father-in-law stopped by to check on us, and when my husband came to, he took him the doctor to have him looked at. We were afraid he had a concussion or something."

"My partner and I are going to take a look around to make sure he's still not lingering in the area, and we're going to have to take the shovel and gloves for fingerprints and DNA. If we're gone by the time your husband and father-in-law gets back home, he'll need to come to the station for a statement just as soon as he is able. In the meantime, you and your kids stay inside and keep the doors and windows locked and don't let anyone in that you don't know."

"Thanks officer, we've already locked the windows and had the doors locked until you arrived."

"Don't hesitate to call if you see anything, even the slightest bit suspicious."

Then I remembered, "Our phones aren't working right now and neither is our electricity. Do you have any idea how soon the lines will be repaired?"

"All I can tell you is that they are working on them, we're all hoping it won't be long. It's a nuisance for a lot of people and it really complicates things when we're trying to investigate criminal activity. Like I said, we are going to look around for a bit. We'll let you know when we get ready to leave and give you a report, so you can put your mind at ease."

I went back into the house and started gathering candles and oil lamps in case the electricity wasn't working after nightfall. I prayed that it would be back on by then. It would be terrifying to be in the semi-darkness with a criminal on the loose, especially one that was after us.

While the police were still looking around, John and Ben came home from the doctor's office.

I rushed out of the house to meet them.

Ben was still acting light headed, so John and I led him to the porch and sat him in our new rocking chair.

"What's going on? Why are the police here? Has something happened?"

"Ben, they think that your injury wasn't an accident."

About that time the officer that spoke to me, came back to the house when he saw Ben. He immediately began questioning him.

"Mr. Hoffman, how are you feeling?"

"I'll be alright. I'm a little dizzy right now, but the doctor thinks it will clear up in a couple of days. I got a pretty bad bump on the head and he thinks I had a mild concussion."

"Do you remember anything about what happened?"

"Well, I remember that the storm was getting really bad, and I was rushing around trying to get the animals inside before it got worse. The rain was turning to hail and the winds were picking up something fierce, and limbs were flying everywhere. I didn't feel like I could make it safely back to the house, so I stayed in the barn with the animals."

"Did you notice anything out of place in the barn?"

"No, like I said, things were pretty hectic, and my concern was only for the animals. I thought at one point, before I was hit and blacked out, that there were some footsteps behind me, but I figured it was the animals moving around. I didn't think much about it. Should I have been concerned?"

"Like we told your wife, there had been a prison break and the man who escaped was the one who kidnapped you and left you for dead a few years back."

"So you think he's back to finish me off, or get revenge for my testimony that put him in prison?"

"We are looking at that for a motive, yes, but it may have just been a coincidence that he happened to take shelter in your barn during the storm and you were in the wrong place at the wrong time and rather than being caught by surprise, he knocked you out and ran."

"Is my family or me in any danger now?"

"I would stay as close to home as possible until we catch him. We've looked around your place and don't see any evidence of him anywhere around, but since he doesn't have a vehicle, at least that I'm aware of, he could still be in the area. If you have to get out or work around the farm, it wouldn't hurt if you took someone with you. Do you have a neighbor that can help you out for a few days?"

"I don't know of anyone. We thought about hiring a farm hand, but we haven't done it yet. Maybe my father could loan us one of his for a few days," Ben replied.

"I was just going to suggest that," said John as he overheard the officer as he stepped onto the porch. "You're not going to be in any shape to work for a few days anyway. I'm sure Caleb wouldn't mind helping you. You two have always been close. I'll still have Jeremiah to help me out. We'll get by."

"Thank you, as long as you are sure you can spare him."

"I'll send him over as soon as I get home," John said.

"I'll get the guest room ready so he'll have a place to sleep, if he decides to stay with us," I frowned.

"That will probably be a good idea at least for tonight or until we catch this guy," the officer added.

After John left to go home, Ben and I sat out on the porch for a few minutes longer with the police officer. I went inside and got Matthew and the girls and came back out on the porch so they could be with us. The electricity was still down and the cooled down temperatures after the storm along with the slight breeze was a welcome relief to the stale hot air in the house.

"Dat, does your head still hurt?" Deedee frowned.

"Not too bad anymore, sweetie. It will be okay."

"That was a bad man that did that to you, Dat."

"Now, Deidre, it's not our place to judge people. That's God's job to do that. People aren't bad, they just do bad things and God expects us to love and forgive them. He wants us to help them seek a better way and bring them to repentance."

"But I don't like him, Dat."

"We need to pray for him, honey girl, and we need to pray that he will find remorse in his heart and want to clean up his evil thoughts. After all, he may be more afraid of us and the police than we are of him," Ben continued.

"That was one of the hardest things I had to learn to do when I became a Christian and joined the Mennonite church and married your dat. I was full of hate and distrust of people. There were a lot of people I didn't like when I was growing up and I did some things that I wasn't proud of. I had to ask forgiveness of my sins, and for hurting your mammi and dawdy Edgerton when I did bad things. But Jesus, through his mercy forgave me, so I need to pass that forgiveness along to others," I added.

"Besides, if we keep thinking bad thoughts about people, it just makes us feel worse," Ben smiled at the girls. "Life is so full enough of disappointing times, without harboring bad feelings against others as well."

"So, Ben, what would you do if your attacker came up on this porch at this very minute, what would you say to him?" the officer asked him.

"Well, providing he wasn't in the process of attacking me, I'd ask him why he disliked me so much as to hurt me or my family, then I'd try to resolve our issues."

"If he didn't listen, what would you do next? What if he came at you and threatened to harm your family?"

"Assaults against me are one thing, but against my family are something else. A man needs to do what he can to protect his family. If reasoning and prayer doesn't get results, then I may have to fight or get him under control by force, but that should always be a last resort."

"You have a lot of faith and patience, Mr. Hoffman, but I wouldn't be quite so forgiving and restrained if it were me or my family," the officer stated. "Some people are just born evil and there is no reasoning with them. Our jails are full of them. I've lived in the Amish and Mennonite community nearly all of my life, and it never ceases to amaze me, how you all can be so laid back when it comes to the bad things of this world."

"Well, the Bible says we are to be set apart from the world and live for him," Ben replied.

"Unfortunately, we people outside the faith, live in the 'real' world where evil is all around us. As a policeman I see the worst of humanity every day. I wish sometimes, I could be more like you all."

"Officer, are you a Christian?"

"I would like to say so. I grew up in a Christian home, but I'll have to admit that after I left home, I quit going to church. Just didn't see any point in it," he frowned.

"To be Amish, or a Mennonite like us, you have to totally surrender your will to God. Like I said, you have to set yourself aside from this world. Any Christian, for that matter, needs to put their complete faith in God and not in this world. I grew up in an old order Mennonite home. Our lifestyle is close to the Amish in our ways, in that, we interact with our friends and family as a close-knit community and we wear similar type clothes…"

"But, I notice you have cars and trucks instead of horse and buggies like your neighbors and you have a phone and electricity."

"That is one thing that sets us apart from the Old Order Amish. Some of the newer, more modern Amish have those things as well. You'll notice that our vehicles are all black, including the bumpers. We use the vehicles out of convenience and for work. They are not something to be worshipped or loved. Although we have electricity and a phone, again as a convenience, we haven't got a television, computer, or cell phone. We feel all of those things would distract us from worshipping and putting God and our family first," Ben said.

"It's not impossible to become like our people," I told him. "I grew up in North Carolina in a "so-called" Christian home, too. We went through the motions, especially around the holidays, with going to our church, but God was never the center of our lives. When I came to stay with my great grandmother, in this very house for the summer seven years ago, I was introduced to her Mennonite faith and her church. It was difficult at first to give up everything I thought I loved, like TV and the Internet and all the modern conveniences, but then, I realized that I could totally live without those things and I gave my life completely to God and the church, I never went back to my old lifestyle. I also met my husband during that time. My newfound faith grew along with my love for him. I was thankful that we shared that faith."

"So, say I wanted to join your church, what would I need to do?"

Ben smiled. "To become a Christian, you don't simply join a church, like you do an organization or club. You can come visit our church anytime you want. We don't turn anyone away, even if they are there out of curiosity. We do get visitors all the time, but to join the church you will need to become a believer. You need to confess your sins to God and accept Christ as your savior as you would in any other Christian church, following that, if you want to become a Mennonite or Amish, if that's what you want, you would need to take instruction and learn the precepts of their faith and you would need to accept those precepts and take them into your heart and home. You would need to be willing to give up worldly things so that you can be fully immersed in the faith. It is difficult for most people to be willing to do that."

"Thank you. You gave me a lot of things to think about."

About that time, Caleb pulled up in the driveway.

"Well my relief is here, I'll feel better knowing you have someone to stay with you. Thank you for our little talk. I'll check back with you tomorrow."

CHAPTER 9

SINCE THE ELECTRICITY was still off, I went to the kitchen and sliced some bread and made up a plate of cold cuts and cut up vegetables and fruit. Sandwiches would have to be our supper this day.

We decided to sit outside to eat. Since the windows were still closed and locked up, it was warm and stifling inside. We cleaned off the picnic table and spread the sandwich fixings and iced tea out for everyone to dish up their own. Caleb kept a close eye out for any would be prowlers on the farm while we tried to enjoy our meal.

We talked to Caleb about our long and eventful day. We had a wonderful day at market. It was great getting back in touch with Sarah and Ezekiel and the children got to meet each other and become friends. I looked forward to seeing them again. They were Amish but they had no issues with being friends with us, because they were more modern in their thinking, and since we were more conservative, our values were actually very similar.

I was pleased with how many of my rag dolls I sold. They were very popular. I made some without faces and wearing Amish clothes for my friends of that religion, but they were popular with the tourists as well. I also made some wearing brighter clothes or flowery prints with aprons for my Mennonite friends and visitors. My girls loved it when I worked on the dolls. They helped me pick out the material to use and the colored yarn for the hair. I had a sewing machine to work with, but I preferred to stitch them all by hand in the traditional way. It kept me in practice making stitches for when I assisted the other ladies in working on quilts.

I had also sold several jars of preserves. They always went well with the tourists. Ben had made a few doll beds, and some customers bought them to go with their new dolls. He sold some produce from our farm. We always had fresh corn, tomatoes, green beans, and cucumbers from our plentiful garden. In the fall, we would bring bushels of apples along with canned applesauce and apple butter.

Our day at market was cut short by the threatening weather and storm after we arrived home. It was a scary time for us, but even scarier was finding my husband unconscious on the barn floor after being attacked by someone. Thankfully, God was good, and he would be all right and the storm did no serious damage to the farm. It just inconvenienced us by knocking out the electricity and phone.

Now as we finished eating our supper, we talked about the events of the day, and how they shaped our lives.

Then we told Caleb how we were able to witness to the policeman, and his interest in how to be saved.

"It truly is amazing how God can use the different situations that happens to us to further his kingdom," Caleb grinned.

"I was thinking that myself. We might never had the opportunity to speak to him, had I not been attacked," Ben added.

"You reckon he'll show up to church tomorrow?" Caleb asked.

"I don't know, but it will be interesting to find out. Well, Caleb, I guess we'd better do a quick walk through on the grounds and make sure all the animals are in for the night. The sun will be setting soon, and we don't need to be wandering around after dark, not after what happened today."

While the men were checking on the farm, the girls and I brought the dishes into the kitchen. I put Matthew in his highchair while I did the dishes. The electricity was still out, so after finishing cleaning the kitchen, the girls and I went to all the windows to open them for a brief time just to let a cross draft through the house to cool it down some before we went to bed. Deidre and Anna were such good helpers for a four and three year old.

I had pulled out oil lamps and candles earlier in the day and proceeded to get them all lit before the sun set for the day.

I was startled when I learn a loud crash just outside the kitchen window. I don't know why, but I looked at Mattie about the same time I heard the loud noise. I was surprised when he didn't even flinch or look around. He continued to sit and play with his toy I left on his tray to occupy him.

Deidre came running down the stairs with Anna at her heels followed by Mittens.

"What happened, Mamma?" Deedee had a terrified look in her eyes.

I looked out the window and saw a large limb that had fallen. That must have been it. Caleb and Ben were outside looking at it. "Looks like a limb fell, sweetie."

We ran outside.

"We're lucky that it fell the way it did," Caleb said. "If it fell a few degrees another direction it would have taken out part of your kitchen wall, including the window."

"That was a blessing, jah?" I said.

"God watched over you with that!" Caleb added.

"I would say that God was good to us all day today, not just with this limb!"

"You're right about that. We're all still alive and our families are safe and our houses are still intact!"

"Now, if only our lights would come back on!" Ben grinned.

"We're spoiled, Ben. Wasn't that long ago, our families didn't use electricity," Caleb smiled

"Thank goodness that's changed."

Caleb knew all about not having electricity. His family was Old Order Amish and when Caleb made his decision not to join the church when he was an older teenager, he started going to the Hoffman's Mennonite church. That is where John and Linda met him and offered him a job working on their farm. They paid him a small amount for spending money and offered him free room and board.

Caleb was two years older than Ben, and when he had started working for the Hoffman's as a teenager, they became fast friends.

When I was staying with my Grand that summer and a storm much like the one we had this day came through and messed up the porch, Caleb was the one who came with Ben to repair it. He was quite the handyman when a job needed to be done.

We had no sooner finished investigating the damage from the falling limb, when the lights and phone finally came back on. It was so good to see clearly again after the dim light. We set about blowing out the candles, extinguishing the oil lamps, and closing and locking all the windows again.

After everything was locked up tight, Ben and Caleb sat to play some dominoes at the kitchen table while I got the children ready for bed and set out our clothes for the worship service the next morning.

I heard the phone ring and Ben answered it. His mamm was checking up on us to make sure everyone was okay. I took a lot of comfort in our relationship with his parents. They were always so thoughtful and concerned about our welfare. I'd like to say the same thing about my parents, but they didn't think about family and our traditions the same way as Ben's folks. Of course, they lived several hours away, and to their credit, they had no clue about what we had been through that day. Maybe I would call them later or tomorrow after church to let them know what happened today.

I turned down the bed and shook out the pillows in the guest room for Caleb. I wanted to make sure the room was comfortable for him.

After I said their prayers with them, I put the children to bed and returned to the living room to spend the rest of the evening with the men. I pulled out my knitting and started working on a scarf. I wanted to make several before the fall and winter markets. They had been great sellers in the past.

I listened as the men chatted about some of the things they did when they were young. I certainly hoped that little Matthew and any other sons we might have don't do all the things they did growing up. I don't know if I would survive all their antics if they were anything like their dat and his friends.

Before going to bed we had our usual evening devotional and praised God for the way he had carried us through the day, and we said another prayer of thanksgiving for seeing Mattie through his illness and prayed for a healthy baby to be born to us in a few months.

Early the next morning Caleb and Ben went to the barn to feed the animals and milk the cows. It was Sunday, but the animals still needed to be tended to. When God created the world and its animals, it's a shame that he made them to continue to be hungry even on Sundays! But when you're a farmer life doesn't stop, even for the Sabbath. Even Jesus said in Luke 13:15: *Thou hypocrite, doth not each one of you on the Sabbath loose his ox or his ass from the stall, and lead him away to watering?"* We'll if Jesus acted like it was all right, who are we to argue.

I made a large breakfast of pancakes and sausages while the guys were out. I wanted to make sure everyone had enough to eat. Church sometimes ran a little long and we were going to have a dinner on the grounds following church. There wasn't always enough to go around by the time we dished up our lunch so I wanted to make sure we all had full stomachs before we left.

After breakfast, I helped the girls get ready. I pulled their fine hair into a bun and pinned their prayer kapps in their hair. It was always a struggle to keep their hair up. By the time they got through running around playing with the other children, half of their hair was loose and flowing down their backs and their kapps were barely in place.

At the lunch several people came up to us and asked about what happened the day before. Evidently the gossip mill had been running full speed. It seems everyone knew about the attack on Ben.

Since it was our first day back after Mattie was in the hospital, several people were interested in how we were faring after that ordeal, as well.

I looked around the fellowship hall, trying to see if our police officer was in attendance, but I really didn't expect to see him there. I guess I was just hoping. I didn't recall seeing him at the service either.

We sat and ate with Ben's parents and Caleb and they brought Jeremiah, their other farm hand with them. He had only recently started working with them and we didn't know too much about him. Through our conversation, we learned that his parents were Old Order Amish and during his 'rumspringa' in his early teen years decided that the restrictions of his family wasn't something he wanted to live with the rest of his life. He was a strong Christian and rather than totally abandoning the church, he chose to join the Mennonites just like Caleb, before him. They were the least restrictive of the two religions and that appealed to him. His family wasn't happy with his decision, but since he hadn't become baptized into their faith, he wasn't shunned from seeing them and he went home to visit them often.

After our church lunch, we all headed to my in-laws house. After all the excitement and struggles of the day before, it seemed nice to be able to get out and visit again.

As usual, the girls headed straight to the gazebo to play while Matthew was content to stay on the porch with us.

At one year of age, Matthew was just now starting to take a step or two. He'd been walking a little more before his bout with the measles, but his illness seemed to set him back a bit. Another thing that concerned me was that he was quieter than usual. He had started to say a few words and tried to repeat some things that we tried to get him to say. Now his only vocabulary was Mamma and Dat, and would look at us strange when we said anything else to him.

While the guys visited and walked around the farm, Linda and I sat in the rockers on the porch and visited while we watched the girls play.

"So how are the new baby and your pregnancy progressing?"

"I'm feeling a little better now, I'm suppose to go to the obstetrician this coming week to make sure everything is okay. I've finally gotten over the morning sickness, thank goodness. When I had time to think on everything, I figured out that I have to be at least three months along. That would make sense since the sickness has almost passed. I don't know why I didn't think about it before."

"Well, you have been under a lot of stress, I can understand with you having so much on your mind. So, are you hoping for a boy or a girl this time?"

"Of course, it don't matter none, as long as it's healthy, but it would be nice to have a little bruder for Mattie. They would be close in age, just like Deedee and Anna are."

"That would be nice for them too, but the good Lord knows what's best, jah?"

"That's what I think, too. Since the doctor warned me about what could happen since I was exposed to Mattie's measles, I'll just be thankful to not have any complications."

"Well, I'll be praying for you. You know that."

"I know, denki. I'll let you know what the doctor says after my visit with him."

Mattie started getting fussy, so I got the girls and went to the barn to get Ben and Caleb. I think we were all getting ready for a nap, because no one seemed to mind that we cut our visit short.

With the children down to rest, I pulled one of the books off the shelf in the living room. My great grandmother had quite a collection of the old classics from when she was growing up and they were left with the estate after she had passed away. I especially loved the books by Jane Austen and Louisa May Alcott. I could read their stories over and over and never get tired of them. I guess I was a romantic at heart and sometimes I would imagine myself as the heroine of one of those novels. Of course, if I thought about it for very long, I'd realize I was living out my own epic tale right here in my own home. Maybe someday I would write my own tale for the entire world to read. Wouldn't that be something!

I must have fallen asleep while I was reading and thinking, because the next thing I knew Ben was waking me up to tend to Mattie. He was crying and Ben tried to comfort him so he wouldn't wake me up, but he wouldn't get still.

"I think he needs his mamma's touch, jah?"

I grinned at him, bless his heart, I know he tried but sometimes bopplies just wanted cuddling from their mamms.

When I got up to go to the kitchen I passed a comical sight. Caleb and Ben were sitting at the dining room table having a "tea party" with Deedee and Anna. I had to smile when I saw those grown men trying to hold the tiny children's tea set with their large fingers and pretending to eat imaginary cookies.

"When I get Mattie settled, I'd like to join you at your tea party and I'll even bring you some of my tea and cookies. Would you like that?"

"Oh yes, Mamma!" Anna grinned, and Deidre agreed.

"That sounds like a plan to us!" Ben winked at the girls.

I felt bad that I hadn't been spending enough time with the girls. Matthew was taking most of my attention with his illness, and babies naturally required constant care even when they were well. I was glad that the girls had each other for company and that their father was good about playing with them when his chores were done. Now with Caleb here to help, he had a little more free time.

Over the next few days things seemed to calm down some. We hadn't seen any sign of strangers about the place, but it was too early to let our guard down just yet.

CHAPTER 10

I WAS NERVOUS and excited at the same time when Ben and I went to the obstetrician together. I was glad his parents agreed to drop by and babysit the children, so Ben could accompany me.

Dr. Zook had been the doctor that delivered all of my kinner and I felt very comfortable with him. He was a member of our church and a good friend of Ben's parents. I was glad that he let Ben in the examination room with us. He said that he actually encouraged the husbands to take a role throughout their wives pregnancy.

When we sat down in his office, he immediately brought up my history of my exposure to my son's measles. "Mrs. Hoffman, your son's pediatrician has told me about his illness and how closely exposed to him you were throughout your caring for him both at home and in the hospital."

"I couldn't very well not taken care of him, ain't?"

"Of course you had to. I also learned that you had no idea that you were pregnant at the time."

"I was in the hospital with him at the time, and the doctor recommended I do a pregnancy test, because I was having morning sickness. He told me the dangers of being pregnant and my exposure to my son's measles and that I needed to see you right away."

"I'm happy that you did. You do have some things going for you though: you're healthy and have had three normal pregnancies, your medical record indicates that all of your vaccines are up to date and even though you've been so close to your son and haven't shown any symptoms lets me believe that you have a strong immune system. The most dangerous time for miscarriages is in the first three months, and if it's true that you think you are that far along, we may be almost out of the woods for that danger. I don't want to get your hopes up that nothing can go wrong, but it looks pretty good right now. I do want to caution you to not get too stressed out over things and you do need to take it slow and easy. No need to take chances. Right now, I don't see any reason why you should be concerned about the whole measles thing."

After taking my history of my monthly cycles, and examining me and listening to the baby's heartbeat, which he proclaimed as sounding healthy, he said that I was more than likely over three months along. He said he'd know more after he did the ultrasound the next month.

Ben and I left the doctor's office more happy and confident than when we went in. I dared to finally get excited about my new little one. We even stopped by the fabric store to get some soft baby flannel, so I could start making a few clothes for him or her. While I was there I also picked up a few remnants so I could work on some more dolls for the next market and begin a new baby quilt.

We stopped by Ben's parent's house to pick up the children on our way home. We were eager to share our good news with them that everything was looking good.

Our excitement was quickly subdued when we were met at the door with my frowning in-laws.

"What's wrong?" I asked, startled to see their expressions. "Are the children all right? Was there an accident? Did that man come around again?"

"Hold up girl, it might not be anything. Neh, the children are fine, at least as far as we know, and there hasn't been any sign of our intruder. You need to come in and have a seat, though."

"What's going on? Please tell us."

"It's Mattie."

Ben and I quickly sat down. "What's happened?" I gasped.

"Have you noticed anything different about him lately?" Linda asked.

"What do you mean?"

"I mean with him not talking much or ignoring everything you say unless you are looking directly at him, or he doesn't respond to loud noises, even when they are next to him? He was sitting in his walker in the kitchen when I dropped a plate close by him and he didn't even flinch. He's not walking like he use to either."

"What are you trying to say, you think Mattie might have lost his hearing and his ability to walk?" I frowned.

"I don't know, I'm not a doctor, but I think you ought to get him checked into. I remembered that when my daughter, Kari, was small she had a little friend that had measles, and later on she became deaf and blind and they found out that she had formed a brain tumor as a result of the measles virus that moved into the brain. You should take Mattie back to the doctor for a checkup and let them look at him."

"I have wondered about his hearing too, but I didn't think too much about it, I figured he was just too preoccupied with what he was doing to pay attention to what was going on around him, couldn't that be what's happening?"

"Well, like I said, I'm not a doctor and I can't tell you what to do, but if it were me, I'd have him checked out."

"Denki, Mamma, it would probably be a gut idea. He actually has a follow up visit scheduled for the week after next, but I'll call and let the doctor know what is happening and see if he can see him sooner."

"I'm sorry to scare you like that. It may be nothing but the fears of an old woman. Try not to worry too much, the good Lord knows what each of our futures hold. I'm sure he will take care of Mattie, no matter what happens. Now then, you looked like you were happy when you came to the door, before I opened my big mouth. What did the doctor have to say about you?"

"He seems to think that everything will be okay, but he did warn me not to get too stressed out over things, but that's not going to be easy, especially with a criminal running around trying to hurt our family and now, this problem with Mattie."

"Samantha, we will pray continually for all of you. Remember to put it all in God's hand. There are things that happen to us that we don't have any control over and no matter how much worrying we do we can't change one thing. Prayer and submission to God's will is what is needed by you right now."

"Denki, Mamma, I'll try to remember. "I have my new wee one to think about now, as well."

It was almost suppertime by the time we got home. I had made an extra large pot of chicken stew the night before so I had plenty enough leftovers to warm up for tonight. I was glad that I thought to make extra so I wouldn't have to cook.

I didn't eat much. After what mamma said, my stomach was tied in knots worrying about my baby bu. I only wanted to hold and comfort him and love all of his problems away.

I gave him some of the broth from the soup and then prepared his bottle of milk. I excused myself from the table and carried him up the stairs to the nursery. After his bath, I sat and held him while feeding him his bottle. I knew he could actually hold it himself, but I needed this time with my son.

As we sat quietly in the room, I cried and prayed over him. Sometimes I observed him tugging at his ears and then as I was speaking my prayers he would touch my lips. *'Was he trying to tell me that he couldn't hear?'* I shook one of his rattles just behind his head close to his ear, and he didn't turn his head or try to take it.

I was still in his room when the girls came in to tell us goodnight. They saw me praying with tears in my eyes.

"Mamma, is Mattie going to be okay? "Deedee asked. "Mammi and Dawdy Hoffman said that he might be sick again. Is he sick, Mamma?

Anna added, "Does he have the measles again, Mamma? Can we touch him?"

"No girls, he's not sick like that anymore. It's fine for you to touch him and love on him. I think he'd like that."

The girls took turns giving him hugs and said goodnight to him.

"Girls, when you say your prayers tonight, make sure you say an extra one for your bruder, okay?"

"Yes, Mamma, we will."

They walked from the room hand in hand after we said our goodnights.

I continued to rock him until he fell asleep. When he looked comfortable and stayed asleep, I crept out of his room and padded across the hall to my bedroom and found Ben kneeling beside the bed, praying. I knelt beside him and put my arm around his heaving shoulders and knew that he was just as distraught over Matthew's condition as I was. After we finished praying, we climbed into bed and into each other's arms and stayed that way until the morning.

As much as we wanted to stay in bed and continue to wallow in self-pity, there were things that we needed to get done. When you own a farm and have a family, life doesn't stop because of the setbacks. I remembered what Mamma Linda said about letting God take care of our problems, so I tried to put a smile on my face and carried on like nothing was wrong. After breakfast I would contact the pediatrician and see how quickly we could get Mattie in to see him, but that would be the end of what I could do for him. The rest was up to God.

The doctor wanted to see Mattie as soon as possible, so we set up an appointment that very day.

I called Linda and John to see if they would mind watching the girls again and of course they were delighted to have them over to the house. They acted like they enjoyed having them around. I don't know what I would have done if I didn't have such a willing baby sitter so close by.

After I washed the dishes and a load of clothes and hung them out to dry, I started a new loaf of bread dough from my sourdough starter. It would take a few hours to rise, so I figured it would be ready to bake when I got home. I also set out a roast to thaw for our supper. It would be ready to be cooked with carrots and potatoes when we got back from the doctor.

The girls were excited to be going back to their Mammi Linda's house. Dawdy John promised to make them a swing to be hung from one of their large maple trees. He said he might even let them play in the sprinkler if they were good. Of course, their mammi also said that she might just be making their favorite chocolate chip cookies and they could even help her, and promised them that they could bring some home for all of us.

As the day wore on before his appointment, I started worrying again. What if my little boy was deaf? What if he had a tumor or had suffered irreparable brain damage? What if he kept getting worse and eventually lost his sight and his ability to walk? What if it was God's will to make my child an invalid? How would I cope?

"Lord, I don't know if I could take what you have for me and my boppli's future, I cried out."

'Be still my child and know that I'm your God. I will not give you anything that you can't handle. Trust in me and I will give you peace'" I heard the voice from deep inside me.

From the time I heard that voice, I knew that no matter what happened that afternoon that God truly would take care of my baby bu no matter what the outcome of the visit to the doctor.

While we were sitting in the waiting room, Mattie became fussy again and started pulling at his ears. I held him tight and tried to comfort him the best I could. But nothing seemed to help.

After we'd been there for a very long half hour, we were finally called back to he examination room. I didn't know how the doctor was going to examine him while he was being so agitated, but he seemed to settle down when he was set on the table. We told the doctor about how Mattie acted like he couldn't hear, and he had stopped walking like he did before. We also expressed our worries about whether or not he could have developed a tumor or something following his measles.

The doctor looked at his eyes and mouth and felt for any swollen glands and checked his muscle reflexes before centering in on examining his ears. He held a tuning fork up to each ear, but Mattie didn't respond to it. After finishing his examination and looking in both of his ears, he sat back in his chair and looked at us into our frightened eyes.

"Mr. and Mrs. Hoffman, I have good news and bad news…"

I clutched Ben's hands. "Tell us doctor. We're ready."

"The good news is that I don't believe your son has a tumor. His muscle reflexes and pupil responses seem to be normal."

"And the bad?"

"He has swollen glands and he has a lot of fluid behind his ear drums. So much so, it could be the cause of his discomfort and inability to hear. It could even be contributing to his disequilibrium preventing him to be steady on his feet."

"So what do we do?"

"I'm going to go the conservative route for a few days and put him on an antibiotic. I want to see him back in a few days to recheck him. If the swelling and fluid haven't gone down by then or if he gets worse,

I'll refer him to an ear surgeon. If it doesn't clear up with medication, he'll need to have surgery to drain the ears."

"Will that hurt?"

"If he has to have it done, he will be put to sleep. He won't feel anything. Then he'll stay in the hospital for a few hours afterwards. But let's think more about that when the time comes. Let's see what the medication does first, and if it comes to it, the ear surgeon will explain the rest. After he is treated, he'll be back to hearing and walking all over the place and driving you all crazy getting into things again."

I had to smile after that comment, because it was true, but I was looking forward to Mattie being his old self again.

"So did this come up because of his measles?"

"I don't have a doubt in my mind. Measles has a definite respiratory component to it and any respiratory disease can affect the inner ears. I'm sure you noticed the runny nose and watery eyes while he was sick."

"I did, and he looked miserable."

"His ears are making him feel bad right now. So it wouldn't hurt to give him some pain medication along with his antibiotics, but please refrain from trying to do anything to clear the ear canals out your selves and try to keep water out of his ears while he is being treated. You could make the infection worse. Right now, I'm going to have the nurse irrigate his ears with a mild antibiotic ear solution and I'll see him back in one week. I'm going to go ahead and set up a tentative appointment with the ear surgeon, just in case we need to take the next step. We can always cancel it, if he gets better."

He gave us the prescription for the medicine and then the nurse walked in with an irrigation tray and a small bottle of medicine with a dropper. After putting the medicine in his ears and draining them, we were free to go.

We felt a little more light-hearted when we left the office and Mattie seemed a little calmer. He acted like he felt a little better. He fell asleep on the way back home and when Ben had stopped by the pharmacy, we waited in the truck so we wouldn't disturb his rest.

After getting the medicine, we went by Ben's parent's house to pick up the girls and to give them the news that Mattie should be okay and didn't have a tumor after all. That was wunderbaar, gut news, as the Amish would say.

It would be great if the medication could help him, but if he had to have the surgery, we could live with that too, as long as we knew he didn't have anything as serious as a brain tumor. God had been with us as he said and we praised him that evening in our prayers.

CHAPTER 11

LATER THAT WEEK, Ginger finally went into labor with her pups. Ben had set up a private place in the utility shed with lots of rags that she could rest on and be away from the prying eyes of the children. Although giving birth, especially on farms, was very common, I didn't want to have to spend my time trying to explain it to the girls and I didn't know how they would feel watching Ginger go through the pangs of childbirth. We decided that it would be best to wait until the pups were here and their mama had a chance to clean them up.

While we were waiting on Ginger's babies, the girls and I had a playtime together. We read in some of their picture books and then we drew some pictures. I told them to draw a picture of Ginger and Mittens and Ginger's babies. That seemed to satisfy them for a little while.

Just before supper, Ben came to get us. The puppies were ready for viewing now. I cautioned the girls not to touch them no matter how tempted they were.

We crept into the shed, and saw Ginger lying as still as she could while her babies were fighting over her teats to get the best ones for milk. Seeing them like that made me miss nursing my own baby bu and looking forward to my new little one in a few months.

"I know you want to touch them, but you'll have to wait until Ginger lets you," instructed Ben.

"They are so cute Dat! Can't we keep all of them?" begged Deedee.

"Now, you know what we told you. You children can keep one, when they get a little older we'll let you decide which one you want, but then we'll have to give the others away as soon as they are weaned. You can enjoy them in the meantime. Just don't get too attached to them, okay?"

"I wonder what kind of dog she mated with." I said.

"Dat said there was a border collie that had gotten loose from one of our neighbors a few months ago. There's a possibility that it was him. That would explain the white and black on some of the pups. If that's the case, they may turn out to be good work dogs for someone," Ben added.

After feeding and putting the dog to rest for the evening we returned to the house to eat.

Matthew had awakened and was crying. I hurried to him and took him out of his crib to take care of him, and noted that he was feeling warm. I started to panic as my thoughts turned to his recent illness, but I took comfort in knowing that he was getting antibiotics and with a little Tylenol, he'd be soon set to rights again. The fever was more than likely the ear infection.

After giving him his medicine and bottle, he finally settled back down and I brought him down to join the rest of the family while we ate our supper.

The next morning I called his pediatrician when he continued to show signs of distress, to tell him about Mattie's fever the previous night and he said to go ahead and make an appointment with the ear specialist. He needed to see him as soon as possible. Thankfully, he was able to see him that very afternoon.

I called Linda and John and, of course, they agreed to watch the girls again. It bothered me to no end that I had to impose on them so much, but they insisted it was no problem at all and they actually enjoyed keeping the children.

I tried to stay busy before the appointment. I kept Mattie near me as I worked in the kitchen and garden. Deedee and Anna helped where they could. If they weren't actually helping me with my chores, they would help by keeping Mattie company and trying to get him to laugh by making faces at him.

The weather was a little cooler this morning and it was a good day to work outside. It had been a few days since I tended the vegetable garden and it was surprising how fast the weeds had taken over. I'm surprised they didn't kill the plants around them by stealing all the moisture and nutrients from the soil.

Then I thought that it was like that with life too, we let all the small things in life that tend to grow like weeds, crowd out what's really important like serving our Lord and allowing him to produce the real and good fruits in our lives. It was strange how even working in a simple garden like this could call to mind the teachings of Jesus.

After the girls and I finished the weeding, we gathered all the vegetables. There were plenty enough green beans, field peas, and tomatoes to do some more canning later today or tomorrow, depending on how everything went at the doctor's.

While I worked in the garden, Ben cared for the animals and then gathered some ears of corn from the cornfield. He wanted to have several bushels to sell at the market this coming weekend. We also had plenty of tomatoes coming on and I figured we'd have enough left after canning to be able to sell some of those as well.

After the outside chores, I began working on the kitchen. I still had the dishes to wash and the wooden floors to scrub. I also made a chicken pie. I figured I could reheat it for supper after we came home from the doctor's.

After all the work was finished, we ate our lunch of sandwiches and fruit and we cleaned up and changed into clean clothes and headed for Linda and John's house to deliver the girls.

Then we headed nervously to a doctor that we had never seen before, hoping beyond hope that he could fix our Mattie.

When we arrived at the doctor's, we saw his name on a plaque next to the door, 'Dr. Hezekiah Beiler, EENT, Specializing in Children's Diseases'.

"I guess we must be in the right place," I grinned.

"Hmm, I wonder if he's related to Ezekiel," Ben said. "Seems like Zeke said something about his dawdy being a doctor."

While we were in the waiting room, we had to fill out a lot of paperwork since we were new patients. Because we didn't have any insurance, we had to provide proof of someone who would cover expenses or give them the bank information for our home and car. We called Ben's parents and they talked with the receptionist to let her know they would vouch for us.

It was often hard for people in the Amish and Mennonite community when sickness came because they didn't like to seek out interventions by the medical community except in emergencies, preferring to care for their families at home. Many, if not most, didn't have any commercial insurance, but did contribute to a community health fund that the members could utilize if needed. We were members of that community, and knew that in a pinch, we could count on them to help. Also, by utilizing the Amish and Mennonite doctors, they would often give us a major discount in their services or provide a way for us to make payments.

"Dr. Beiler will see you now," smiled the nurse. She led us back to the room, where he was waiting on us.

As with Mattie's regular pediatrician, we began by going over his recent history, and Dr. Beiler also looked in his ears, throat, nose, and eyes and felt for any abnormal swelling in his neck.

"His eardrums are extremely inflamed on both sides. He has a large amount of fluid or pus behind them. I know Dr. Smucker had put him on antibiotics a few days ago, but it is obvious it's not helping any. We will have to do surgery and do it as soon as possible or his eardrums could rupture and will be difficult to repair. He could even lose his hearing completely. I would like to go ahead and admit him tonight to the hospital if possible, so he can have the surgery the first thing in the morning. If you wish, you can go home first and do what you need to do, but we will have to get him admitted and get his paperwork and labs done before supper."

"How long will he be in the hospital doctor?" I asked.

"If everything goes okay, he should be home by tomorrow evening."

"So what exactly are you going to do?" Ben asked.

"We are going to do a procedure where we make a tiny incision in the eardrum and suction out the fluid that is behind it. Then we are going to place a tiny tube in the hole, so that air can get into the middle ear and any fluid can drain out. It is called a tympanostomy. It is so tiny you won't be able to see it and you will probably even forget that it's there. We are going to do it in both ears because it looks like both ears are affected."

"It sounds painful," Ben winced.

"He is going to be put to sleep for the procedure and won't even know what's happening. It will only take about a half an hour once he's out. After surgery he will go to the recovery room and once the anesthesia wears off and we watch him for a couple of hours he should be able to go home. He will feel much better and start hearing again right away. Once the pressure in his ears is equalized again, he will be able to stand and walk around again without feeling dizzy and falling a lot. While the incisions and tubes are healing up, we're going to continue him on antibiotics for a few days, and he should be good to go after that."

"How long will he have to keep the tubes in?" I asked.

"They are pretty good about staying in on their own, but after about six to eighteen months they will fall out as the eardrum heals.

They should be okay, but if you were to suspect that there is a problem, you can make an appointment to see me and I'll check him again. Also when you bath him or if he were to go swimming, you might want to put ear plugs in his ears to keep water from entering his ear canal."

"Will he have to have these tubes the rest of his life?"

"No, children usually outgrown this problem, I don't foresee Matthew needing them once these are gone."

"Thank you doctor, you've set our minds at rest. We're just going to make a quick trip to the house to get the girls settled at their grandparents and we'll be at the hospital within the hour," I said.

We dropped by the house and packed up a few things for the girls and an overnight bag for us. We instructed Caleb to watch over things at the farm and do what needed to be done with the animals in the morning, and then we took the bags for the girls to the in-law's house and said our goodbyes and headed to the hospital with Matthew.

After settling in the hospital room, the lab technicians came in a got some blood samples from him. After they were through, Ben went to the cafeteria to get us each a sandwich and chips and a large glass of tea. The nurse brought in some baby food and a baby bottle of milk for Matthew. It would be his last meal before bedtime and his surgery in the morning.

I was restless during the night, I worried about Mattie and his being put under anesthesia the next day and the cot I was laying on was terribly uncomfortable. Ben let me have the cot and he tried to sleep in the armchair with his head resting against the wall. When I glanced at him, he was sound asleep. I don't know how he could sleep like that, but he seemed to be resting better than me.

Early the next morning, even before the sun came up, the nurse came in and offered us a cup of coffee and a snack. She said they'd be up from the OR to get Matthew shortly, and she figured we'd better get a little something to tide us over until they were finished.

We quickly got up and dressed and ate our snack and in no time at all, two of the OR techs were in our room to take Matthew down to surgery.

We were able to go with him to the pre-op room. Bless his heart, but he looked terrified. I so wanted to pick him up and hold him, but it wasn't allowed. The nurses were busy starting an IV on him to give him his medicine to help him relax and fall to sleep. Then they carried him back to the room and we were left and shown to the waiting room. We bought another cup of coffee from the vending machine and waited.

It seems like we were there for hours, although it really hadn't been long at all. After about forty-five minutes Dr. Beiler came out to greet us.

"It took us a little bit longer, because we wanted to make sure that we got most of the fluid out of his ears. He had quite a build up behind his eardrums. It's a good thing we got it when he did. They were almost to the point of rupturing. I'm surprised he wasn't constantly screaming out in pain. I think you are going to notice quite a change in him now. Like I told you in the office we are going to keep him on the antibiotics for a bit longer, but he's going to be okay. There's no reason you can't take him home in a couple of hours after most of the anesthesia wears off. He will probably be sleepy most of the rest of the day, but tomorrow you will have your little boy back and stronger than ever and getting into everything."

"That is wunderbaar, gut news!" I smiled. "Denki!"

Later that afternoon we dropped by Linda and John's house and picked up the girls and went home. It was good to be back home and have all our kinner in one place again.

I was glad that I had made the chicken pie the day before. All I had to do was pop it into the oven for supper.

That night we gathered for our evening devotional and prayer. I held Mattie on my lap and he seemed more calm and happy. I praised God for healing for our son with the doctor's help. It was time to get back into the routine of normal living again. At least it was normal for a little while.

CHAPTER 12

Autumn

THE MINUTES AND hours had turned into days and weeks. As the first cool breezes of autumn had overtaken the warmth of the summer, we started looking into redding up our house for the cooler weather.

Matthew was completely well now and was running all over the place. It was so hard to keep up with him. He loved to chase the chickens and keep them stirred up. It didn't help that the puppies were following him everywhere, including into the chicken coop. Ben and I had to continually run after all of them and keep them from agitating the chickens so much.

Our typical day started with all of the children climbing out of bed and coming to wake us up, that is, if the rooster hadn't done it already. After they brushed their teeth, I dressed them in fresh clothes and put the girls hair up in braids. Matthew's hair had finally started growing out and was starting to become curly, like his mamm's. He would soon need to have his first haircut.

Caleb continued to stay with us, because the police still hadn't caught the intruder that tried to kill Ben. Caleb had become such a great helper to Ben, that when it came time to go back to my in-laws house, he would be missed terribly.

While I was busy cooking a rather large breakfast for my hungry family, Ben and Caleb would take the children to the barn to feed all the animals and milk the cows. I watched through the kitchen window while they did their work.

I can't believe that just seven years ago, I was eating breakfast with my great grandmother in this very kitchen, and the most handsome man I had ever met in my life came to the door, reporting for work on Grandy Dee's farm. Now that man belonged to me and was the father of our three beautiful children and I was pregnant once more. I patted my belly just as the boppli kicked me.

"I don't blame you, sweet child. I know you want to play with the others. It won't be long now, just three more months."

After everyone washed up for breakfast, we had our morning prayer time before we ate. A few minutes later we heard someone drive up. It was the police. I heard him talking into his walkie-talkie as he came up to the door and knocked.

Ben went to the door. "Can I help you officer? "He asked.

"I hate to disturb you while you folks are eating, but I wanted to give you an update on your case. Sorry I've not been around sooner, but there hadn't been much to say. Have you seen anything at all? Anybody poking around that normally isn't here?"

"No it's been pretty quiet, of course, we've had a lot of things happening around here with a sick child among other goings on, so I haven't really been looking for anything. Should we be concerned?"

"Some of your neighbors been saying that they've been missing some of their produce that they've been trying to get together for market. That's been the main thing. Others thought they saw someone skulking around their barns at night, but could never really catch anyone in the act. Bottom line is, we have never captured the man that attacked you, and so you'd better not let your guard down for one minute."

"Thank you officer for letting us know. We've tried to be careful, but like I said we have a lot going on right now. I still have Caleb here to help us and he'll probably be around at least through harvest."

"Folks around here think that he may be possibly trying to find a place out of the weather, since we started having cooler nights. I don't know if he'll try to come back here or not after the trouble he gave you, but you can never be too careful."

"We'll keep an eye out and let you know if we see anything suspicious. Thank you for dropping by."

After breakfast everyone went back to their chores. Market was in just two days and we had apples and pumpkins to pick and some apple butter to can. I had a few of my dolls to finish up and I had made a few capes and aprons ready to sell. Ben and Caleb had brought in quite a haul of fresh corn and we had several bushels ready to sell.

The girls helped me most by keeping an eye on their little bruder and keeping him occupied while I was trying to cook and clean.

After the market this weekend, I would spend the next week cleaning out the cupboards and washing the curtains and quilts to get ready for winter. The rugs also needed to have the dust beat out of them, but I would have to get Ben and Caleb to help with that. I didn't want to do that much heavy lifting with the new baby and all. Mopping floors and cleaning baseboards on my hands and knees and picking up baskets of wet laundry were about the heaviest work I wanted to handle right now.

My heart went out to little Matthew as I watched him play with the puppies. In two days he would have to chose just one and the others would be sold at market. They were all so cute, it would be hard to get rid of any one of them. I worried, too, about Ginger. I prayed she wouldn't grieve the loss of her pups too much, but I knew we would never be able to keep four large dogs after they had grown.

The pup would be Matthew's dog. The girls were content to have Mittens as their pet. As much as they liked the puppies, I think they were always aware that they would have to say goodbye to them, and that Mattie would be the primary child to keep the dog, so they just never became that attached to the puppies.

After lunch, I started a pot roast over a low heat so it would take most of the afternoon to cook and I cut up some potatoes, carrots, onions, and celery to add later when it was close to being finished. By then I was extremely tired from all the work I did that morning. The baby felt like it was turning somersaults in my belly, so I told Ben I needed to lay down for a bit and gave him instructions to keep an eye out for the children. He was fine with that especially since it was almost time for their naps, as well.

After a good two-hour nap, I woke up to a quiet house. It was almost too quiet. I jumped out of bed to see what was going on. That's when I saw that the truck and my family were gone and so were three of the puppies.

I made a quick trip to the bathroom before going downstairs to put the vegetables in with the roast. I was shocked when I saw that I had started bleeding. It wasn't a lot, but enough to get me upset. It must have been all the heavy work I had done earlier that day. I started cramping, and I remembered what the doctor had said about miscarriages and premature births. Could it be that I was getting ready to lose my baby?

I needed to call the doctor and I needed to get back in the bed, but the supper had to be prepared too, so I put the vegetables in with the roast and I called my in-laws hoping beyond hope that Ben was with them. Linda might know what to do. I could talk with her while I was on the line.

"Samantha, you need to get off your feet and contact the doctor, it's way to early to have the baby. You need to take care of yourself!"

While Ben and the kids were on their way back home, I called the doctor.

"I was a little afraid that this might happen, Samantha," he said. "But I thought we were beyond the danger time. "I want you to stay in the bed the rest of the day and see if the cramps and bleeding stops. If it doesn't, I want you to get to my office the first thing in the morning. We need to find out what's going on. Has the baby been moving around?"

"Yes, I felt it earlier today. It was very active."

"What about now?" he asked.

"Not so much, but I feel it every once in a while."

"That's a good sign, but like I said no more work for the rest of the day. Your husband will have to take care of your other kids. You need your rest. Actually, I would like to see you in the morning, even if you are feeling better. We'll go ahead and do a sonogram on you to make sure the baby's okay."

"All right, doctor, we'll be there first thing. Thank you."

About that time, Ben and the children came back home. They found me in the kitchen sitting at the table.

"What are you doing up?" Ben asked.

"I had to get our supper. I still have work to do."

As I sat there, the tears came to me and I laid my head down on my crossed folded arms and cried.

"Mammi, it's okay, Dat and I will take care of you," Deedee said, as she patted my back.

"You need to go lie down now. You know what the doctor told you. The baby is the most important thing for you to take care of right now. We can finish the supper and the dishes."

"The laundry is still on the line, too, and the market is the day after tomorrow. We need to go to that so we can get some money!"

"Again, we'll take care of it. We'll take care of you."

"Where are the pups? Has someone bought them?"

"Believe it or not Mamm and Dat decided to take two of them. Isn't that great? The children will still be able to see them and Ginger can visit them anytime we take her over there. We will only have one left to sell at the market. I'm sure someone will take him."

Fresh tears came to my eyes. "I'm going to miss them."

"I know, but like I said at least we will be able to see them again. Who knows maybe one of our friends will take the other one and we will be able to visit that one too."

Another round of cramps came again, so I decided I'd better get back to bed. Ben helped me up the stairs and there I stayed until my doctor's appointment the next morning.

The bleeding and cramping had almost stopped by the time we drove to the doctor the next day, but it still worried me to no end.

I was glad when they called me back to the examination room almost immediately so I wouldn't have to stay up any longer than needed.

The doctor examined me and did the ultrasound. The cool gel and scanning rod sliding across my skin made my muscles contract and my boppli jump in my womb.

I watched the monitor as he looked over every nook of my little one.

"Your little one looks healthy right now, but there may be a slight tear in your birth canal because he's tried to push his way into it and it caused a tear. The smooth muscles in your womb are weak due to having your children so close together and it's not holding him as well as it should. You may have to stay in the bed the rest of your pregnancy or at least be where you can keep your feet up, and there will be no more lifting heavy objects until he is safely delivered. Also as much as possible, avoid stressful situations."

"You keep saying 'he', are you saying we're having a son?" Ben asked.

"I'm sorry, I should have asked if you wanted to know the sex of the baby. I guess I let the cat out of the bag," he smiled.

"That's okay. It didn't matter what the sex was, we were hoping it was a boy, but after all we went through, we just wanted it to be healthy."

"I want to see you back in two weeks unless you have any further problems. We'll re-evaluate your need to stay in bed at that time. It could be that you'd be okay doing some lighter things, but just not right now. If you can get some help that would be great."

I felt much better after the doctor visit, but I honestly didn't know how I would get things done. It was unfair to add any more work onto Ben's already crowded workload, and what about the market tomorrow? I dearly wanted to go and see my friends again. It was one of the highlights of my week.

I was feeling quite a bit better on Saturday, market day, and the bleeding had stopped. I promised Ben that I would stay sitting while we were out and he finally agreed that he thought it would be okay, as long as I stayed put and didn't try to get up and do things. I could just sit and watch, and he would do all the heavy lifting and selling.

Several people came to our table and we sold several things. It helped that we had the puppy on a leash close by and all the children dragged their parents over so they could get a closer look at him and then the parents ended up buying something while they were there.

Deidre and Anna came running over to our table from the playground with their friends, Rachel and Rebekah, to show them the puppy. Of course, Sarah had to see what all the commotion was with her girls, and she was interested in seeing her friend again. This gave her the excuse she needed to leave her table for a few minutes to come over to where I was sitting. When I didn't get up to greet my best friend she came closer to speak with me.

"The girls seem to have taken a shine to your pup, is it for sale?"

"It is, you interested?"

"Zeke's been interested in getting a watchdog, especially with all the break-ins happening lately. Of course, I don't know if he'd be interested in a pup. Still the girls seem to have fallen in love with it already. How much are you asking for it?"

"We were hoping to get fifty dollars, but you are the first ones that have expressed an interest in him. I'm still anxious to get that second porch rocker from you. Maybe we could trade like we did the last time?"

"Jah, let me get Zeke ove'r here to see if he'd like to get him and make the trade for him, if he's interested, that is. How come you are sitting and not selling?"

"The doctor's got me on total rest right now. I'm having some problems."

"Ach, do you think it was because of Matthew's being sick and you being exposed to him?"

"The doctor doesn't think so, I'm just having some problems carrying him."

"Him? You having a boy?"

"Jah, we are excited."

"Congratulations! We hope to have another baby, but it hasn't happened yet. Maybe soon God will bless us with another little one."

"I pray for that for you, Sarah."

"We'll I'm going to go back to our table and I'll send Zeke over so he can see the dog. You can send the girls back with him. We'll be leaving to go home in a few minutes. There aren't many customers out today. I guess the cooler temperatures are keeping them away."

"I'm sure we won't be far behind you. I'm getting tired and I probably need to get off my bottom and lay down for a while. Don't need to overdo right now."

A few minutes later, Zeke came over and talked with Ben about the pup, and walked away with it still attached to its leash. Their girls were ecstatic. I was happy they were the ones to get him because that way whenever we visited, we'd be able to see him again. My children were sad to see him go, but they, too, were happy that their friends would be his owners.

Zeke brought the porch rocker over to our table and I knew that it was the payment for the pup and I was so happy to finally have the complete pair of rockers for the porch.

After packing up all of the food and items we didn't sell, we headed back home. It had been a slow day, and I wish we would have had more customers because we had a lot of food left over that would need to be canned before it went bad, and I knew I wouldn't be able to be on my feet long enough to get it done. My mother-in-law said that she would drop by to help out, but I knew that she had a lot of her own foods to put up as well. So we decided on a plan. She would come to my house and do the lifting and canning part, while I sat and shucked and cut the corn off the cobs and cut up the green beans and squash. At least that was a job that wasn't too demanding. Our overabundant cucumbers would make some fine pickles and I could sit while I sliced those, as well. Then we'd finish off what we didn't sell of the apples and make some apple butter and canned pie filling. Then after we were through at my house, we would go to her house to finish up her canning.

In the meantime the men would work together to do all the chores at both houses and between the four of them, including Caleb and Jeremiah, they would help keep the three children corralled. The men also cooked the meat outside on the grill and Mamm and I would cook what was leftover of the vegetables we were canning to go with the meat. Altogether, we felt like it was a great plan, and for about a week, it was.

But soon, all our strength and all of our faith and power of forgiveness would be tested once again as our life was soon to be thrown into the darkness of evil itself.

CHAPTER 13

"Samantha, you shouldn't be out of bed this morning, you know what the doctor told you," Linda chided.

"I'm going crazy laying around so much. I need to be doing something to help around here."

"Well, the doctor thinks you need to stay as rested as possible these last two months. He wants to give your wee one the best chance to be healthy, especially after the scare you had a few weeks ago."

It had been a month since I had the pregnancy scare and I had slowed way down from all the housework I had been doing. I decided to put off the rest of the major fall housecleaning until after the baby came. My mother-in-law spent part of her days with me, especially helping with the day-to-day housework, laundry, and cooking. Then she would return to her house to do her chores there. When she cooked, she would make extra so she could feed both of our families.

I continued to have mild contractions, so the doctor wanted me to be on bed rest most of the time now, but it was difficult with three young children demanding my attention. I didn't know if I was going to make it two more months.

While I was up, I decided to eat my breakfast out on the porch. It was a beautiful fall day and I enjoyed the crisp air and autumn leaves that were so lovely this time of year. The falls were pretty in North Carolina, but it couldn't beat the beauty of the colorful maples in our area.

The children were already through with their breakfast and were running around the yard playing with the puppy and the kitten that was almost fully grown at this time. It was a joy to see Matthew so healthy looking and happy. He had started running all over the place now as he tried keeping up with his big sisters. I smiled as I watched them laugh and play in the piled up leaves.

Deidre would soon be turning five and would soon be ready to go to school the next year. She was already such a smart little girl and was growing up way too fast. She was so protective of her younger sister and brother and such a help to me, especially in the kitchen. She loved to help me cook. *'After the baby comes, I'll have to spend more time with her.'* I thought.

"A penny for your thoughts, Samantha," Linda said, as she came out on the porch to join me with a second cup of tea.

"Just enjoying the kinner and the fresh air and our new rocking chairs. You reckon, heaven will have anything this beautiful when we get there?"

"Ach, this and more! Just think, we will have no more pain or tears and there will be no bad things to happen to us and best of all we'll be with Jesus every single day! What a blessing that will be, ain't"

"Jah that it will be."

"Linda, it is so nice, having you around to keep me company like this, you've been such a wunderbaar, gut help to me. I don't know what I'd have done without you these last few months."

"It's been my pleasure, truly. It's nice to feel useful and welcome. I'm so happy that Ben chose you to be his wife. He couldn't have done any better. I honestly didn't know how I felt about him dating an Englischer girl at first, but when you joined the church and started following our ways it was easier for us to accept you and then when you two discovered you were actually already a part of my family, I couldn't believe it!"

"We were excited when we found out that you were actually my mamm's cousin," I grinned.

"Ach, that made some lively conversation around the dinner table at that first reunion," she recalled, laughing.

"People were shocked to think that I was going to marry my cousin," I smiled, remembering the conversation.

"That's before they learned that Benjamin was my stepson and not a blood relation. Besides we never even knew I was your mamm's cousin until you and Ben found those pictures in your great grandmother's attic. I had been adopted as a baby and never knew my real mother until we were introduced at that family reunion seven years ago when you were staying with your great grandmother, who happened to also be my own grandmother."

"A lot has happened since that time," I said, looking over at the barn and the children running to meet their father and Caleb.

I was proud of my home and farm. Ben had taken such good care of the house and barn. They were over one hundred and fifty years old, being built around the time of the Civil War. My great grandparents bought the farm shortly after World War II, and my great grandfather used the barn to start a furniture business and worked in it until his death a few years later. Grandy Dee continued to work the business hiring both Amish and Mennonite carpenters to continue the work he had started. Even my great uncle Freddie worked with them until he joined the Air Force in the late fifties.

After the business shut down, it was used for what it was originally intended for, to house farm animals, and store some of the crops that were harvested.

Before we met, Ben would come over and help my great grandmother with the animals and do any repairs she needed on the house and old barn. He did a wonderful job keeping up with it. The old red barn had seen many years and with Ben's help and care would no doubt see many more.

With sitting up for so long, I started to have a few cramps again, so I decided that it would be good to lay down for a little bit. I really didn't want to go back to bed, so I rested on the sofa and propped my feet up on pillows. My ankles had a tendency to swell this late in my pregnancies and propping them up always seemed to help.

I picked up my Bible and opened it to a random verse. It fell opened to a verse in Romans 12:19 that seemed to speak directly to me: *"Dearly beloved, avenge not yourselves, but rather give place unto wrath: for it is written, Vengeance is mine: I will repay, saith the Lord."*

What on earth? *'Why are you telling me this, Lord,'* I prayed. Am I still holding evil thoughts about the man that tried to kill my husband? Is this why I've been having so many problems with my pregnancy? Is my body reacting to some deep-seated anger? Have I been harboring anger toward my parents or toward those I grew up with and not realized it? Whatever, it was, I would pray for forgiveness.

I closed my eyes, still clutching my Bible and prayed fervently for God to remove any stumbling blocks to having perfect peace with him and others in my life.

After praying, I fell into a deep and peaceful sleep and forgot about the pain I had been experiencing a few minutes ago. I had been asleep for a few minutes when all of a sudden, I felt something land on my protruding abdomen. I looked down and saw Mittens curled up, and asleep. I'm surprised the baby didn't wake her up, because as soon as she was comfortable, the baby started doing somersaults inside my belly. Mittens must of thought she was being massaged because she started purring.

We must have been a comical sight when Ben and his dat came in a few minutes later, because when I woke up again they were standing over me, smiling.

"What's so funny?" I asked them, smiling back. "Can't a pregnant woman with a cat on her belly look ridiculous without being laughed at?"

"Actually you look adorable, Samantha," Ben grinned. I need to take a picture of this so I can keep this image of you for all time."

"Ha, ha, very funny," I said, and as I started to get up, the cat jumped off my lap and ran out the front door to hide in the barn. "I guess she didn't like being laughed at."

After my 'cat' nap, I got up for a little bit and worked on my baby's layette. I still had some clothes from when Matthew was born, but I wanted our new baby to have some of his own clothes as well. Winter was coming and I was knitting a new blanket and sweater for him. There were so many things to do to prepare for our new little one.

Ben had taken the baby crib that Mattie had outgrown out to the barn. He was going to strip the old paint and varnish off of it and re-stain it so it would look like new. He wanted to do it away from the house due to the fumes. Because it was getting late, and he thought he would need the better part of a day to complete it, he decided to start on it the next day.

It was getting close to suppertime and the sun would be setting soon, so Ben and Caleb decided to fire up the grill to cook. My in-laws had gone back home to get a few things done at their house, but planned on returning for supper. She was going to bring potato salad, homemade rolls, and corn on the cob to eat with the barbecued meat.

Later, while we were sitting outside at the picnic table, Ginger and her puppy, Marmalade, whom we christened 'Marmie' and Mittens stayed at our feet, begging for their share of the meat. I believe they got more of the meat than we did.

While we were sitting and eating, we heard some noises in the bushes behind the barn. Ginger and Marmie started growling and Mittens perked up and stared in the same direction.

Caleb and Ben ran in the direction of the noise carrying sticks with them and the animals chased behind them, but when they got there, the noise had stopped and they didn't see anything.

They came back to the table with the dogs on their heels. "Must have been a raccoon or some other critter," Ben said. "We didn't see anything out of the ordinary when we got back there."

"Where did Mittens go? She's not here," Deedee frowned.

"She's probably off chasing mice around the barn, she'll return when she gets bored, she always does."

That seemed to calm her fears down a bit. After all, Mittens was never known to stay out all night. She liked her nightly sleep time with the girls too much.

Ben's parents left to go home for the night and Ben and Caleb looked around the barn one last time to see if they could spot the cat and when they didn't see her, they came back to the house. They figured she would come to the house when she became hungry and they left a bowl of food and water out for her on the porch.

We all got ready for bed, and had just settled down for the night, when the dogs started barking something fierce. Ben went for his rifle and met Caleb in the hallway as he started down the stairs. They didn't realize that Deedee had followed them until it was too late.

A faint glow could be seen coming from the barn. It looked as if someone was inside with a lantern. There wasn't any reason for one to be lit inside the barn because it did have electrical lights.

Ben turned to me and told me to call 911. I quickly called, just as I heard him call out to Deedee.

"Deidre Ann, get back here!"

"I have to get Mittens, Dat! I heard her meowing in the barn," she called back to her father while continuing to run towards the sound she heard in the barn.

"I said stop right there!"

But Deedee didn't stop.

After I called the police, I ran outside just as I saw someone in the shadows of the barn reach out and grab my daughter. She tried getting away, but he was holding her too tight, that's when I noticed something in his hand. It looked like a gun!

"You come any closer and your pretty little girl dies," he called out.

I ran to Ben and held him. "Oh my goodness, what are we going to do?"

"The police will be here soon. Just keep praying and please keep the other children back and take care of yourself and the baby. I don't need to lose anyone of you."

"Do you think he'll harm Deedee?"

"I hope not, but if it's him, I've seen what he is capable of from my last two encounters with him, and I wouldn't put anything past him. He's pure evil. If you could see him up close, you would see it in his eyes."

Ben tried to keep the intruder distracted until the police arrived, by talking with him. He took a few steps closer to him.

"Stay where you are, and let me see you throw your gun to the ground or you can say goodbye to your girl here."

"Ben, do what he says, I think he means it!" I cried.

"You have a smart woman there, Ben," he called out. "It actually worked out pretty good that your daughter came running to me! It was pretty fortuitous really."

"You need to leave her out of this, she hasn't done anything to you."

"Well, she may just be the leverage I need with the cops in getting out of here. Besides, if something did happen to her, what a payback I would have!"

"What do you mean by that, payback for what? I'm the one you attacked and almost killed...twice!"

"You're still alive aren't you? I could have easily killed you, but I didn't."

"So why did you try to kill me?" Ben asked as we watched him grip Deidre even tighter while she was struggling to get free.

"You didn't get to hear my story in court, because I was forced to take a plea bargain and say I was guilty when I stole your truck all them years back. Looks like I actually done you a favor, that truck was a piece of crap anyways, and now you have a lot nicer one, but I digress."

"Okay, so now you have my full attention, tell me why you took my truck and held me hostage while you were driving recklessly through the hills and then left me for dead and torched my truck."

"This is what really happened that night. I was at work and got a phone call from my wife saying that she was in labor and was at home alone with my little girl. I became frantic when my car wouldn't start and I happened to see you come by. I knew you wouldn't be willing to take me no fifty miles away, so I took you by force."

"You don't know me, if I would have known the situation you were in, I would've taken you where you needed to be. So why did you force me to strip down and then torch my truck?"

"I already had kidnapped you and stole your truck. I really wasn't thinking straight, I had taken some drugs earlier and I wasn't being too rational at the time. I figured that it was best to get rid of the truck and make you disappear."

"Why didn't you take me all the way to your house?"

"Are you kidding me? You would've learned where I lived and would have sent the cops to get me once you got back home. I couldn't take any chances. I stopped about a half mile from my house."

"So what happened to your wife and daughter?"

"See, that's where it really got messed up for me. When I arrived home, my wife was already trying to deliver the baby. I got there too late and we lived miles from any hospital. I tried to help her the best I could, but I couldn't stop the bleeding. My wife and young'un both died when she gave birth."

"What happened to your daughter?"

"After everything that happened with my wife, I was blamed for not trying to get her to the hospital, they took my daughter from me. Since I was sent to prison for stealing your truck and kidnapping you, she was put in the foster system. I don't know where she's at right now. With all the trouble I got myself in, I've been shunned from my family."

"You were shunned? Were you Amish, then?"

"I was in name only, I didn't practice the Amish faith since I was a kid, I was supposed to get baptized after my rumspringa, but I never got around to it. I'm not so sure I believe all that stuff anymore."

"It's not too late to turn yourself around, even now," Ben said.

"Yes, it is. I've done too many bad things and being in prison has really hardened my heart. Right now I'd just as soon kill you and your family and never look back. I have nothing left to live for, and you are part of that reason since I've been in jail because of you."

"Mittens!" Deedee cried out.

As she yelled out her name, the intruder grabbed Deedee tighter around her waist and put his hand over her mouth.

Mittens became frightened and she jumped from the loft to where the oil lamp was burning close to the crib. She accidently turned it over as she ran past it and out into the yard.

During the next hour I saw the culmination of my very worst fears and nightmares all rolled up into one terrifying scene. Nothing could ever prepare me for what happened next.

CHAPTER 14

THE POLICE PULLED into the yard, followed by another cruiser as backup and an ambulance came shortly behind them. Were they really thinking that someone was going to be injured this night?

The intruder pulled back further into the barn and was now holding a gun to Deidre's head.

The overturned lantern just so happened to be next to the paint and varnish removers and stains from where Ben had been working on the baby's crib. Added to that, there were several bales of hay for the animals stored in the barn close by where he had been working. It didn't take long for the hay to catch on fire and when it reached the cans of paint and varnish, there was a loud explosion. As the barn quickly caught on fire, the animals rushed past each other trying to get out of the blazing inferno. It was difficult to keep our eye on what was happening with our daughter because of the crush of the animals.

The police were calling for the firemen to get there as soon as possible, because of the fire, as they were moving in closer to the barn.

We heard the gunman threaten, "If you come another step closer, I'm going to kill her!"

"Put it down, Danny," I heard the officer say. "There's no reason for you to do this, you can save yourself and the little girl. You can be a hero tonight if you bring her out of the fire and protect her."

"It's no use now. We're both dead and you know it. There's no way out, the fire is all around us now."

"It's not too late, Danny, I see an opening in the fire you can come through. Follow my voice."

"It's too late."

Those were his last words that I heard. All of a sudden we heard a loud explosion that sounded eerily like the sound of a gunshot. I heard myself scream and then I passed out.

I few minutes later, I was being put into the back of an ambulance as the sirens from police cars, ambulances, and fire trucks all blared in unison.

I looked towards the barn that was completely engulfed in flames and prayed that my sweet girl was safe along with all the livestock and I prayed that the fire wouldn't reach the house. Last of all I prayed for our assailant that God would have mercy on him and forgive him, no matter what happened to him.

The EMT's were trying to stabilize me after my fainting spell and they wanted to take me to the hospital, but I refused to leave with them until I found out about my daughter.

I looked over at one of the other ambulances and found them loading someone in the back of their van with a blanket over their face.

I let out a little cry, worried that it was my sweet little girl. That loud noise I heard must have been him shooting her was all I could figure out.

Then I saw a couple of the firemen working with another figure, this one much smaller than the one being loaded on the ambulance. "Deedee," I whispered, putting my hand over my mouth.

Ben came over to the door of the ambulance as they brought the small figure over to rest beside me on the way to the hospital.

Deidre lay beside me as the EMT's were starting IVs on her and keeping the oxygen mask on her.

When I looked startled, the EMT reassured me, "Mrs. Hoffman, your little girl is going to be okay. She had some mild smoke inhalation and a few first degree and second degree burns, but nothing worse than she would have by being in the sun too long. We just want to make sure she's well hydrated and treated for the burns and that her lungs are clear. They will probably keep her overnight, but then she should be able to come back home tomorrow. You, on the other hand, may have to stay a bit longer. Because of the stress you were under, your water looks like it has broke, and you'll probably be going into full-fledge labor before the night is over."

"I'm only seven months pregnant. I can't have the baby now."

"But, nevertheless you will have the baby within the next twenty four hours."

"What about that awful man?"

"He won't be bothering you ever again, ma'am. While the firemen were trying to reach him, a ceiling timber fell on him and knocked him out. Your daughter managed to get away from him when that happened and the firemen pulled her out of the building, but when they went back to get him, he was almost dead. He managed to get out just a few last words before dying."

"What did he have to say for himself?" I asked.

"He asked for your family's forgiveness and asked if you would find his little girl, Cecilia, to make sure she was okay and he also asked God to forgive him for his messed up life. After he said that, he slipped away."

When I glanced over and looked at my young daughter fighting back from her injuries and the terror of the last two hours, all I could think of was what Danny had said about his own little girl. At the time of her mamm's and baby bruder's death, she was probably not much older than Deedee. Then after losing them, her dat was thrown in prison and she was sent to live with God only knows who.

I made up my mind right then, after I recover from my own boppli's birth, and with God's will, his health being satisfactory, I would try to find out what happened to Danny's little girl.

Later that night, the nurse wheeled me down to the pediatric unit, so I could visit my sweet little Deidre. Her dat was sitting on the side of her bed reading her a book.

"You two are a sight for sore eyes," I tried to smile.

"Hey aren't you supposed to be upstairs getting ready to have our boppli?" Ben asked.

"My contractions haven't started yet, besides I had to come visit my honey girl, to make sure she is okay."

"I was so scared, Mamma. That man hurt me and wouldn't let me get Mittens. He was going to kill me!"

"It's over now, sweetie and he won't ever hurt you anymore."

"Dat, is Mittens okay?"

"Yes, sweetie, Mittens ran into the house and will be there to greet you tomorrow when you come home."

"Mamma, will you be coming home with us, too?"

"No honey girl, I have to stay here until your little bruder is born. Then we can come home. How are your burns? Do they hurt a lot?"

"Not too bad, the nice nurse put some medicine on me and made it feel better. Dat, are all the animals okay?"

"I believe they are, Deedee. Caleb is at home now and he is taking them and putting them into a fenced in area where they'll be safe."

"Where are Mattie and Anna?"

"Your mammi and dawdy Hoffman are at our house. They are going to stay until we all get back home. They are very concerned about you and your mamm," Ben said.

"So, Deedee, what did you think about riding in the ambulance?" I asked.

"It was kind of scary, but I'm glad you were with me, Mamma. It kind of hurt when they put the shot in my arm."

"I know it did, sweetie. Look, I have one too," I told her as I pointed to my own IV. They won't be in very long. They just needed to have a place to give us some medicine."

"I know what we can do, while we are sitting here, we never came up with the name for our new little boppli," Ben said.

"You know, you're right. I guess I was so worried that we were going to lose him before he was born, I didn't want to take a chance on naming him and tempting fate."

"So what are the doctors saying now, are they hopeful that he'll be okay after our scare tonight?" Ben asked.

"They did a sonogram when I arrived and listened to his heart, and they said everything looked good. They estimated him to be at least six pounds, so if his lungs are developed enough, he should be okay. So have either of you thought about what you wanted to name our little one?"

"How about Luke, Mamm? Dawdi's name is John and my bruder's name is Matthew, just like the books the in the Bible. We will have Luke and the next baby can be Mark. What do you think, Dat?"

Ben started laughing, "I think it's a wunderbaar, gut name, but your mamm has to agree and I think it's a little soon to be planning for the next one."

"I love the name, Deedee, as long as I can name him after your dat, too. How about Luke Benjamin."

"Sounds perfect, Sam. I like that name a lot." Ben replied.

"Ach," I cringed. "I think I'd better get back to the labor unit. I just had a contraction and it was pretty strong. I think boppli Luke is ready to come into this world."

The nurse came and took me back to the labor and delivery floor and Ben promised me he'd be up in a little bit just as soon as Deidre was settled for the night. After he left her, he came to my room and called his parents. They must have been sitting next to the phone because they answered on the first ring.

"Hi, thought I'd call and give you an update. Samantha has finally started her labor, and the doctor said that everything is looking gut."

"Have you ever decided on a name for him?" Ben's mamm asked.

"We decided to name him Luke Benjamin. Luke was Deidre's idea and Samantha wanted to name him after me, too."

"That's great, son. I love that name. Deedee and your wife picked out a good one. How is she doing by the way?"

"Which one?" Ben grinned.

"Both, of course," Mamm replied.

"Well Deidre is resting now, the nurse gave her some pain medicine and she was getting sleepy when we left her. Her burns weren't too bad and the doctor said there shouldn't be any scarring. Samantha is having contractions every five minutes, so judging from her last three births, I would say it won't be long."

About that time I had another hard contraction, and he stopped talking long enough to help me with my breathing.

"Ben, is everything okay?" I heard her say over the line.

"Jah, the contractions are getting closer now, I don't think it will be long now. How is everything back at the house?"

"The kinner are in bed, finally. It took a while to settle them down after all the excitement. They are worried about all of you, as we are. The police and firemen have finally left and the fire is completely put out. I dread to see what's left of the barn in the morning light."

"I'm sure there will be nothing left, I honestly don't know how I'm going to be able to afford to rebuild it. Nothing will ever replace the memories of that old barn and what it meant to Samantha and her family."

He looked at me and I had tears in my eyes as I thought about the stories Grandy Dee told me about my great grandfather and all the furniture he made in that old barn when it was his carpentry business. Grand would be sad to see this day.

"Is everything okay with the house?"

"Jah, there doesn't look like there will be any danger from the fire and it didn't reach any of the other outbuildings either. The fire was contained to the barn. It's quiet here now except for the sounds of some of the frightened animals. It looks like they all survived the fire. They may be a little spooked for a while, but they should be okay. Caleb managed to get them all corralled behind fences"

"How about Mittens and the dogs? Are they all right?"

"Mittens is asleep in the bed with Anna and the dogs are curled up at our feet, as we speak. They are all perfectly calm."

"That's good to know. Could you do a favor for us? I know it's getting late, but could you call Samantha's parents for us and let them know what's happening and also let them know that she's getting ready to deliver the baby? Tell them we'll call and give them an update tomorrow. They'll be anxious to know. If Mattie and Anna wakes up let them know that we are all okay, and we will be home soon."

"Okay, son. You take good care of our girls. We'll see you tomorrow. Don't worry about us here. We'll be fine. We love you and God bless you all. You'll be in our prayers, as always."

After my next contraction, the nurse assured Ben that it would be a little while longer before I was taken back to the delivery room so he went back down to check on Deidre one last time to make sure she was still resting and then when he was satisfied that she was out for the night, he came back up to stay with me until little Luke was born.

The contractions became closer together now, and I had a hard time resting between each one. They took me back to the delivery room and allowed Ben to come in with me so he could see the baby being born.

After being in labor for another hour, Luke Benjamin Hoffman came into the world, screaming and carrying on like nobody's business. Obviously his lungs were working very well. The doctor checked him over and pronounced him a very healthy six-pound baby boy, and congratulated us. The nurse cleaned him off and wrapped him in a warm blanket and brought him to Ben and me to hold. It was a precious moment for us, and the perfect way to end an otherwise horrific night.

Once I was settled into the mother-baby unit, along with our son, Ben decided to go back to Deidre's room so he would be there when she woke up. It was important for her to know that her dat was with her. It also gave him a chance to catch a brief nap in the chair in her room, as well, after the long restless night. I know he had to be exhausted, as I was, but at least I had a bed to sleep in.

I was finally able to get a couple of hours of sleep before Luke woke up and he already wanted to nurse. Since I'd been through this three other times, they didn't have to come and instruct me, I just went ahead and picked him up out of his bassinet and put him in bed with me. I always enjoyed this time with my wee babies.

The nurse came in shortly after I got back in bed with him. "Good morning, Mrs. Hoffman, I see you are already up and nursing your son. I just need to check you over to make sure everything looks good and then you can eat your breakfast. Dr. Zook will be in a little later to check on you and your baby."

"Thank you, nurse. Other than being a little tired. I feel fine. Baby Luke seems to be doing okay too."

"What a cute name. He's a little sweetheart. I'm glad everything turned out okay. We were worried about him coming so early and all."

"My family needed a blessing in our life after what happened to us last night."

"I heard about the madman and the fire on the news this morning. That must have been an awful experience for you."

"My daughter is on the pediatric unit. She was held hostage with a gun held to her head until the gunman was hit in the head from a fallen timber and knocked out. She suffered some burns when she was taken from the fire."

"Wow, I didn't know that happened. How awful! Well, you certainly deserved to have the blessing of a healthy, beautiful baby!"

"Jah, in spite of everything that had happened, God was good to us. My family is safe now. Our home is intact and someday we will be able to rebuild the barn and life will get back to 'normal'."

"Bless you and your family, Mrs. Hoffman. I pray that life will be wonderful for you from now on."

"Please, call me Samantha."

"My name is Angela, I'll be your nurse for today and tomorrow, too, if you are still here, that is."

"Oh, I doubt they'll let me go home today. Not with just having my baby four hours ago."

"I don't know about that. It doesn't seem possible, but they've started letting people go home the same day or a day later for a while now. It's not like the old days when women stayed in the hospital for a week. Times have changed. I guess they figure the women can rest easier in their own homes and beds."

"Ach, we will know when the doctor sees me, I guess."

Close to lunchtime, Ben came in to visit, bringing the children, including Deedee riding along in a wheelchair, since she was still a patient. They were anxious to see their baby bruder.

"Ach, he's so tiny!" exclaimed Anna, her eyes big with excitement. Can I hold him?"

The nurse in the room spoke. "It probably wouldn't be such a good idea for the children to be handling him right now, maybe after the doctor checks on him later to make sure he's okay and you take him home."

I looked at Anna, with tears in her eyes. "That would probably be best, sweetheart. We'll be home before you know it and we wouldn't want anything happening to him that will make our stay any longer, jah?"

"Okay, mamm. Just come home as soon as you can! Mittens and Marmie misses you too!"

"And I miss them too." Then I turned to Ben, "How bad did the barn look this morning?"

"Unfortunately, as we expected, most of it's gone. The foundation is intact since it is concrete, but everything else will have to come down and either be burned to ashes and plowed under, or taken off somewhere before we can even think of rebuilding. Some of the unburned parts of the timbers, we might be able to cut up into firewood for the winter. No point in letting anything go to waste."

"Winter will be upon us soon. What will happen to the animals? They will need shelter from the cold."

"I've been making some phone calls to some friends of mine. A few of them said the larger animals like the horses, cows, pigs and goats can be boarded on their farms until we rebuild, we just have to get them there. I think I can rebuild the chicken coop and duck yard easy enough, so they can stay with us. Their enclosure wasn't too badly damaged and it won't take much to fix it."

"Please keep the children away from the ruins. I'm sure there are a lot of things they could get hurt on."

"We all have to stay away from it right now. There is police tape all around it while they are in the process of investigating what all happened, since it is basically still considered a crime scene. It will be a few days until we can do anything. Anna and Deedee are old enough to realize they can't get in there, but we're keeping our eye on Matthew. You know how he is when it comes to running around and chasing after Marmalade and Mittens. He's so uninhibited when it comes to going wherever he wants to go, we have to keep our eyes on him every minute."

"So I guess I lost my baby crib, you were going to fix up for me," I frowned.

"It was completely destroyed, I'm sorry."

"Luke is so tiny, I'm sure he'll be able to stay in his cradle for a couple of months until he outgrows it," I lamented.

"We should be able to find another crib at the thrift shop or at market in the meantime and I can fix it up for him," Ben smiled.

As they were getting ready to leave, Dr. Smucker, the pediatrician, came to the room to examine Luke. Mattie hid behind his dat. He must have remembered him from his measles and ear problems, and thought he was here to see him.

"You don't need to hide from me, Matthew. I'm here to see your little bruder, not you, today. Of course, I wouldn't mind knowing how you are doing."

"I'm gut" was his only reply and we all had to laugh at how bashful he was acting. He was definitely not that way around anyone else.

After looking over Luke he turned to us. "You all ready to take this boppli home today?"

"Do you think he's ready?" I asked incredulously.

"I don't think we can do anymore for him here than what you would do at home. That is, if your obstetrician is prepared to let you go, too. I have already discharged Deidre."

"It would be nice, if we could all go home together, and not have to make another trip over here. I'm ready for my family to all be home and under one roof again," Ben grinned.

Since my doctor hadn't been in to see me, Ben took the three children out for ice cream. I envied the time they had together and longed to join them in their delicious treat. I know Ben had to have been trying hard to help the children, especially Anna and Deidre, to forget the horror of the night before.

CHAPTER 15

ALTHOUGH I WAS anxious to get back home from the hospital, I didn't think that the doctor was seriously going to let me go home that very afternoon, especially with the problems I had towards the end of my pregnancy, but after he examined me, he didn't see any reason why I couldn't go home since I had such a great support system in my husband and my in-laws.

When I arrived home, I was still weak and tired so Ben helped me up the stairs and into bed so I could be closer to the bathroom and Luke could stay in the room with me. Over the next few days the children would often came by to visit the baby and me and I would sit up in bed and read stories with them and help them color pictures. They would tell me tales of their adventures with the puppy and cat and fill me in with all the gossip surrounding their dawdy, mammi, and dat.

Linda stayed with us and did everything I wasn't able to do until I was back on my feet again. I got up and moved about the room and sat in the rocker by the window, holding Luke and nursing him when he was hungry. That was the extent of my mobility for the first few days. Linda or the girls would bring me my meals and anything else Luke and I needed so I wouldn't have to go up and down the stairs. I think they did it just so they could have an excuse to come visit us.

While I was at the window, I had a clear view of the barn or what remained of it. They had finally taken down the police ribbon and Ben and Caleb, along with his dat and Jeremiah, started sifting through the ashes and coals to find any tools and horse gear and farm implements that they could salvage and clean up.

I saw mamm running after Matthew several times trying to keep him away from the area while they were working. I wanted to be out there with him to protect him. I guess it was just the mothering instinct coming out in me.

Later in the day I heard a couple of horse and carriages pulling up in the driveway.

Ezekiel, Sarah's husband, had come in one of the buggies and brought along a few other men with them. Some of them, I recognized from the weekend markets.

My window was open to let in the cool air and I overheard them talking.

"I brought some people to help you, Ben," Ezekiel called out as he walked up to the burned out barn.

I know it had to have been a hardship for the men to come from their own farms to help us out. It was the middle of October and they all should have been on their own farms harvesting their crops and doing their own chores and it humbled me to no end to see the camaraderie of these neighbors. I had never seen this type of friendship before I moved to Amish country when I married Ben, and I was so thankful for it now, especially in times like these.

After a few days, I was up nearly all the time, I had gotten over all of the soreness from the delivery and my body was slowly getting its strength back. I ventured downstairs a little more everyday and was finally able to help Linda in the kitchen with the cooking. Everyday we made sandwiches and tea and lemonade for the men. I know they appreciated it while they were working so hard. Ben was able to salvage some of the farm equipment, but we had lost so much of it in the fire. I didn't know how we were ever going to afford to replace all of it, let alone get the building materials to build another barn.

While the men from the community gathered together the charred wood from the barn to burn it off in bonfires and get rid of the ashes, Ben was hard at work rebuilding the chicken coop and fence for the chickens and ducks, the only animals we had left on the farm, other than the cat and dogs. The rest of the animals were temporarily cared for at my in-laws and a couple of other neighbors' farms until the barn could be rebuilt.

At the end of October, the area where the barn had been was now completely cleared except for the foundation. What was remaining of our crops had finally been harvested and stored in another of our outbuildings and we were looking forward to a quieter winter in a few weeks.

Luke was a month old now and the last checkup with his doctor was a good one. He pronounced him completely healthy. Luke had still slept in our room in his cradle. I hoped he would soon start sleeping all night, so Ben and I could get some more rest.

I started worrying about Ben. Now with the rush of cleaning up the barn over with, and after finishing the harvesting, he started to feel useless. I could see the despair and sadness in his eyes and it made me concerned. He just wasn't his sweet, energetic self that I married six years ago. He'd been fine up until a few months ago when we thought that we were going to lose Mattie to his illness, then the attack on him. Even though God blessed us with another child and he was beautiful and healthy, he became concerned about how we were going to pay for the extra mouth to feed. And there were also the hospital bills, and getting the money he needed to rebuild the barn.

One day, he looked up at me, while he was going over our budget at our kitchen table. "This doesn't look good, Sam. We've got more bills than income right now. I don't know how we're even going to make it through the winter."

"It's gut that we don't have a house payment, ain't?"

"We have that, but if we can't pay for the hospital and our utilities, we may have to sell off some of land and maybe even the house."

"Ach, no. We can't do that. We have to have somewhere to live and besides my great grandmother left us this house to buy. We can't lose the house!"

"And I don't want that either, Sam, but we're going to have to do something!"

"Have you talked to your parents? They would be upset to hear you talking like this."

"I don't want to talk to them about our money problems. They've done so much to help us already. Neh, we need to figure out what we are going to do and where we need to go to from here."

"Maybe I could ask my mamm and dat for help. They actually make quite a lot of money. They haven't done that much for us over the years. Leastwise, not like your folks."

"Samantha, it's not right that we are beholden to anyone. It's not our parents' place to continue to provide for us when we are full-grown and on our own. I've never asked my parents for money. Their assistance was with lending a helping hand with the kinner when we needed it and some produce from their farm. For that help, they freely gave and I have been grateful for that help, but I would never have them give me money. In 1 Titus, Paul says: *'But if any provide not for his own, and especially for those of his own house, he hath denied the faith, and is worse than an infidel.'*"

"So, Benjamin Hoffman, do you have any suggestions of what we can do?"

"Our friend Zeke has been talking about starting a furniture business and he has a lot of orders right now. He says he has so many he can't keep up with the demand. His rocking chairs, like the ones we got from them have been one of his best sellers. He said he'd be willing to train me if I'm interested in helping him. I could work with him and we'd split the profits or at least he'd pay me for the work I'd do."

"How do you feel about that?"

"You know I'm a farmer at heart, but with most of the animals at other farms right now and without a barn to work in and the winter just ahead I guess I could try it, at least over the next few months and see how it works out. Thank the good Lord that we don't have a house payment and we have a lot of our food stored up thanks to you and Mamm. We could get by for a little while. Of course, if we don't pay our electric and telephone bills soon, we may be living like some of our Amish neighbors. You willing to cook on the wood cookstove and wash your clothes by hand?"

"I think I could manage that for a little while," I grinned. "As long as it gets turned back on before the weather gets too hot again next summer."

"Zeke's also talking about starting an Amish furniture and gift shop. Sarah wants to put some of her handmade quilts and such in the store. She said she would welcome some things made by you if you're interested. She said she'd give you the money from what is sold, and pay you, if you're willing to come and help her run it."

"What would I do with the children?"

"Well she plans on having a room in the back of the store where they can play and if you both are running the business, you could take turns watching the kinner."

"I actually think I would like that. I had thought at one time about having a tearoom when we first were married, but since I got pregnant right away, I put it out of my mind. I wonder if Sarah would be interested in having a corner in the store for people to have some coffee or tea and some kind of sweet treat to go with it?"

"Whoa now, slow down. I haven't told Zeke I was going to do it yet, let alone go through all the planning for their shop."

"How about we invite them over for supper one night and we can talk about it?" I smiled.

We were interrupted by three sets of feet coming into the house, followed by Caleb scooting them inside.

"Mamma, Mamma, lookie at what Caleb found!" Anna said, all excited.

"What is it?"

Caleb handed Ben and I a strange metal box that had been wrapped in twine. The metal had rusted and the twine was almost deteriorated but it was still sealed. When we opened it, all of our mouths fell open, including the children's.

Inside there were thousands of dollars all tied up in bundles. There was a note in an envelope addressed to Ben and I.

It read:

'To my darling great granddaughter, Samantha, and her husband:

I can't tell you how much I enjoyed having you spend the summer with me and how thrilled I was when you and Ben fell in love and decided to get married.

During the year while you were waiting to get married, I went to the bank and pulled out all of my savings. There should be close to fifty thousand dollars here. I put it in this box, hoping that someday when you were cleaning out the garden shed, you would find it.

I took a chance, as you can tell, but I somehow knew that my children and grandchildren would see fit for you two to buy this house. I actually had a hand in helping them to decide to do that for you.

Anyway, I didn't want to tell you about the money, but I figured that someday you would be needing a little extra cash to get by on *because we all know that farming doesn't pay a lot, so I left it in the garden shed where you would be sure to eventually find it.*

This transaction is perfectly legal and even though we don't have a lot of dealings with the government and lawyers, I did make sure this letter was notarized and authorized by the bank and their attorneys.

Ben and Samantha, this is my wedding gift to you and your future children. If I know anything at all, I know you'll spend it wisely.

God Bless you, my darlings, and even though I won't be with you much longer, I will be looking down from heaven and listening to your prayers.

Love you forever, from your Grandy Dee.

"Mommy, are we rich?" Deidre asked.

"We are rich indeed, but not just because of the money, but because we have each other, and our family and friends, and a love that knows no bounds, and best of all, we have a God that knows what we need and answers our prayers.

I put Luke down briefly, as we all started hugging and laughing. With God's and my great grandmother's gift we were going to be all right.

"What are we going to do with all that money, Dat?" Anna asked.

"Well, I think we need to use it to get all these bills paid off and then get the lumber so we can rebuild the barn, and the rest, we'll put a little aside for a rainy day, and if there is anything left over," he grinned. "I think we all need to go out and get some ice cream to celebrate!"

"I luff ice cream!" Mattie smiled.

We all laughed with him. It was great to see him happy and talking so much.

"And, I'll even be able to come and get some with you this time," I grinned. I thought back to when I was growing up with my family in North Carolina. We had ice cream all the time at home and thought nothing of it. But now when we went out for some, it was a special treat.

After the children went back outside to play, we called Linda and John to share our good news.

"Dat, it looks like I'm going to be able to get my barn rebuilt! Exclaimed Ben. "Caleb and the girls were cleaning out the garden shed, storing everything for the winter and they came across a metal box that we didn't realize was there. Turned out, Samantha's great grandmother left us several thousand dollars and had put it in that box for us."

"Are you sure that she left it and it wasn't something placed there by some thieves who are planning to return and get it? You can't be too sure about people, especially after what you just went through."

Ben laughed. "It's alright, Dat, there was a notarized note from her. I'll double check with the bank from where she withdrew it, but it all looks legitimate."

"So what are you going to do with it?"

"I don't want to leave it laying around, so I plan to take it to the bank along with the note, and put it in our checking account right away. Then I'm going to pay off the doctor bills and utilities and go to the lumber yard and place an order for the wood to rebuild the barn."

"You know how much you're going to need, son?"

"I thought I'd go and take all the measurements and figure it out from there. I would love to have it built before winter sets in.

"Do you want me to come and help you figure everything out?"

"That would be great. You know more about that sort of thing than I do."

"I have built a few barns in my day, that's for sure. "I'll be right over."

John came a few minutes later, excited to be able to help Ben with his planning. He brought some sketches from the last barn he helped build and they used those as a starting point. After they made the measurements and adjusted the figures on the blueprint, they were ready to start.

Later that day, with money and barn sketches in hand we all piled into the van, and went to the bank to deposit the money and then to the ice cream parlor. After our delicious treat, we drove to the lumberyard and hardware store and Ben ordered all the wood, nails, paint, and roofing supplies to complete the barn. With everything he had to get, we had just enough left to cover the rest of our bills, with a little money left over to get us through the winter.

Our windfall was wonderful, and it gave us what we needed for the short-term problems, but we still needed a regular income for the long haul.

CHAPTER 16

OCTOBER WAS ALMOST over and soon winter would be upon us. It was Monday morning now and the lumberyard manager said they would be delivering the supplies for the barn this coming week.

Ben was anxious to get it built because he was more than ready to get his animals back home before the bad weather set in. It was hard for me to watch him pacing back and forth in the evenings because of not having anything to do. He and Caleb did the best they could to plan it during the daytime, but without the supplies at hand, it wasn't going fast enough for him. 'It will take us forever to get it done, at this rate,' I often heard him say.

Monday evening Sarah and Zeke came over for supper and I was so excited to see my friends again. This was the first time they visited us in our home. They brought their girls and Deidre and Anna were thrilled to have their friends come and visit. They immediately took them up to their room to play with their dolls and the dollhouse. Matthew tagged along, not wanting to be left out. How nice it would be when Luke was old enough to play with his older bruder. I'm sure they would become gut friends just like Deidre and Anna.

Matthew, Zeke, and Caleb walked out to the area where the barn was to be built. I glanced out the kitchen window just as they were walking around the perimeter of the foundation. They stopped to talk every once in a while.

I put Luke down in his stroller, so I could make the gravy for the mashed potatoes to go along with the roast I made for our supper.

"He sure is a purty little boppli," Sarah sighed. "He's so tiny!"

"He was born a couple of months early, but he's growing like a weed now."

Sarah bent over him to make a face at him and was rewarded with him smiling back at her. "Such a pleasant baby bu."

"Jah, of course I think so too, but he sure can get fussy when we are trying to sleep at night," I grinned. "So have you and Zeke thought about any more children yet?"

"Oh, Samantha, such wunderbaar, gut news. I just found out this past Friday that I'm expecting, too!"

I gave her a big hug. "That is wonderful news. Is Zeke excited?"

"He's ten feet in the air! He's beside himself! He wants a large family. Speaking of Zeke, he told me that he talked to Ben about going into the furniture making business with him. Did Ben talk to you about it and about possibly opening a furniture and gift shop?"

"Ben did say something about it. He seemed like he'd be interested in doing that with him."

"And did he say anything about you working with me in the shop?"

"He did, and I really like the idea. I'm not sure I'd be able to work all day, everyday though, there are always so many things to do around here. When Ben gets the farm up and running again, I'll have my hands full, especially with four young kinner running around."

"I'll have three children myself by the time we open and I won't be able to keep it open full time, but it would be a nice change of pace for a few hours each day."

"I think I'd like to do it for a bit and see how it works out. I had another idea and I thought I'd ask you what you think."

"What is it? I'm looking for suggestions."

"Ever since I'd starting sharing afternoon teas with my great grandmother here in this very house, and then visiting with my stepsister-in-law, who happens to own a tearoom back home in North Carolina, I've been thinking about how neat it would be to have a tearoom here, but I don't really have the funds to set up a business like that. When Ben told me what you were trying to do with your gift shop, I got to thinking that maybe we could have a corner or a separate room where we could sell tea or coffee along with homemade baked goods to the customers. It might even help to sell whole pies and cakes and other gifts while they are there. It may even bring in more folks who are there primarily for the morning or afternoon tea and not leave without buying something."

"Ach, that is a terrific idea, Sam. I'd have to discuss it with Zeke, of course, but I love the idea!"

"The only thing is, we'd probably need to get someone to help us watch the children while we are working," I frowned.

"We'll see how it goes, until we get it up and running gut, maybe we can alternate times watching the kinner. My mamm says that she could even watch them, if we need her too," Sarah replied.

A few minutes later, the men came in the house.

"Supper smells mighty good," Zeke announced.

"Pot roast with vegetables, mashed potatoes, homemade dinner rolls, and apple pie for dessert," I smiled.

"Those are all my favorites," Zeke grinned, as he winked at Sarah.

"Glad I made them, then," I smiled back at them.

The children all sat at a separate table, and engaged in child-like prattle while we adults all sat together and discussed the barn and the new business venture.

Zeke loved the idea of having the tea and coffee room at the shop. What a sweet little gift shop and tearoom it could be if we did it right.

Sarah and I could make needlecraft items to sell along with the baked goods, preserves, and pickles, and the men would make some furniture and wooden toys. We would even sell items made by some of the other neighbors on consignment. It would be nice to be able to fill the shelves with homemade things, all made here in Amish and Mennonite country.

I had a hard time going to sleep that night because I kept tossing and turning, thinking about the new venture that my best friend and I would be sharing. When I finally did fall asleep, baby Luke decided it was time for his feeding. So I crawled out of bed to change his diaper and brought him back to bed with me to nurse him.

As I looked down at my sweet boppli at my breast, I thought about the last few days. On Friday, I had never seen my husband so low. He nearly broke down in despair when he thought that all was lost when we couldn't even pay our bills and then finding that money that changed everything. I thanked God that Grandy Dee had thought so much of us that she left us a nest egg, to claim at just the right moment in time. It was almost as if she knew that one day we would have need of it. It was serendipitous that it was found at just the right time in our life.

And our new found friends! What a blessing they had become in our lives. In spite of our minor religious differences, with them being Amish and us, Mennonites, we were pretty much alike. Our beliefs were very similar. We had believed in the old ways for the most part, and we shared our love and faith in God and our love of family and friends. To think that if Mattie had never gotten the measles and had to go to the hospital, I might've never met Sarah and Zeke and we wouldn't be planning on opening a shop and tearoom right now.

I finally drifted off to sleep with my baby in my arms and Ben's arm around the two of us. I snuggled in closer to him as I savored the love I had for my wonderful husband and my little one.

We were all sound asleep when the girls came running into the room to wake us up.

"Mamma, Dat, wake up." Deidre yelled in my ear.

"Shush, you'll wake up Luke. What is happening?" I whispered.

"Mamma, there's a man at the door and a big truck in the driveway!" She tried to quiet her voice down, but it was still loud enough to stir Luke awake. I nudged Ben and when he heard what Deedee said, he pulled on his trousers and went to the door straightaway.

As the children followed him down the stairs to the door, I quickly dressed and pulled my hair up into a loose bun until I could brush it out properly later. I laid Luke in the cradle and went down the stairs to see what all the excitement was about.

Sitting in our yard, was a very large truck with all of our lumber and supplies for the new barn. Ben woke Caleb up and the two of them helped the truck drivers unload all of the wood.

While they were working, I brewed a pot of coffee and made a large stack of pancakes in case the truck drivers were hungry and thirsty after their delivery. It looked like a lot of work unloading the truck.

I fed the children their breakfast, so I could keep them inside and out of the way of the workers. It worked for a few minutes, anyway. I also changed baby Luke's diaper and nursed him and then made sure the children were fully clothed and hair brushed before they ventured back outside.

Then I tried to get myself presentable before I went outside to offer the men some breakfast. They were just finishing up when I finally made my way outside.

"Would you men like a cup of coffee and some pancakes?" I offered.

"That's mighty nice of you, ma'am. I don't mind if we do. All this loading and unloading makes a person awfully hungry. My name is Mason and this here is my assistant, Josh. It's nice to meet you all."

I took the pancakes and coffee and fixings out to the picnic table. They said they didn't want to come inside since they were covered with sawdust and sweat, and to be truthful, I was glad they made that decision, although I wouldn't have fussed if they did come inside.

Ben and Caleb decided to eat outside with them and get to know them once the work was finished.

"You folks have a lot of work to do to get that barn back up. Are you planning on having it done before winter sets in?" Mason asked.

"I'm hoping too, but it doesn't look to likely," Ben frowned. I would at least like to get it done enough so that I can get my livestock back. We had to board them at some neighbors until I have a place to house them."

"I heard about what happened to your barn and your family. I'm glad that feller got what was coming to him and he won't be bothering you no more," Josh said

"I wasn't happy that he was killed in the fire, I wish it ended differently and let the courts sort it out. As he was holding my daughter hostage and then as he lay dying, I learned more about his story and the reason for his anger. I think with a little understanding and God's love he could have eventually turned his life around."

"You're just too kind. If it were my kid he was holding hostage, I wouldn't have even hesitated to blow him away. I wouldn't have waited for the building to fall in on him," Josh continued.

"God will judge him. It isn't my place to do that. He didn't kill us, even though he had the opportunity to do so, and the fire was actually started when our cat knocked over a lantern, catching the hay and varnish remover on fire. It all escalated from there."

"Did you have any insurance to cover your losses?" Mason asked.

"No, never had a reason to have insurance, and we don't really believe in commercial insurance. In our community, the families tend to band together and we all contribute to a fund so that when one family has a crisis, we all come together to help them," Ben replied.

"It's a shame, that folks on the outside of your faith don't have something like that, sounds like a better plan than paying outrageous fees into insurance companies. Most of the time all we're doing is making the companies richer and we hardly ever, if at all, need their services. At least you guys know where your money is going to and it helps support your friends and family."

"We were fortunate that Samantha's great grandmother left us some money that we were able to use for this. We didn't have to depend on our friends and neighbors for this problem. It would have taken too much of the reserves."

"So do you have anyone to help you build this thing?" Mason asked.

"Well there's Caleb and me, and my dat and his farm hand might can help after they finish getting in their crops. Harvest is almost over, so they should be able to help some."

"There's some builders that come into the store that might could help, for a fee, of course," Mason smiled.

"Thanks, I'll keep that in mind if it looks like we'll need some help," Ben replied.

They started to get up from the table and nodded to me. "Thank you Ms. Hoffman for the coffee and food. It really hit the spot."

"You're more than welcome. We appreciate your bringing our order so quickly. We wasn't expecting it quite so soon."

"Hope we didn't inconvenience you coming by so early."

"That's quite alright, it was time for us to get up anyway," Ben grinned.

The men got in their truck and headed back down the road.

After they left, I went back into the house to do the dishes and the laundry. With four children and a husband, the clothes and dishes were a never-ending chore. After the load of clothes was washed, I headed out to the clothesline to hang them up. As I was finishing them, Anna and Deidre were chasing each other around under the clothes.

"Girls, where is your bruder?" I asked them, looking around.

They shrugged their shoulders. "I thought he was with Dat," Anna offered breathlessly, as she started chasing her sister again.

I stopped them from running. "Deidre, have you seen Matthew with your father?"

"No Mamma, it's been the longest time. Dat is busy with Caleb putting the wood away."

I ran over to the men. "Have you seen Mattie?" I asked, frowning.

"No, I thought he was with you! Wasn't he playing with the girls?"

"They thought he was here with you!" I became frantic by this time.

I kept the girls with me as we started searching around the house and yard. The girls and I stayed close to home, and searched the entire house and fruit cellar. We even thought about the attic, but I know he couldn't have gotten up there without help.

After determining that he wasn't in the house, we looked in the garden shed and utility building and we even looked inside the chicken coop. While we were looking near by the house and garden, Ben and Caleb started scouring the fields and nearby woods. After not finding him, I called Linda and John and told them to keep their eyes out for him in case he wandered over to their place. I couldn't imagine a one and a half year old going that far from home, but I was getting desperate now and grabbing at any straws I could think of.

"Have you called the police, Samantha?" Mamm asked.

"I did and they are on their way over here. I'm so afraid, Mamm! I don't know if I could stand it if anything happened to my sweet boy."

"Samantha, John and I are coming over, I don't think you and the other children need to be by yourself right now. Let us come and help."

"Denki, Mamm, that would be most appreciated for sure."

After I hung up the phone, the police were at our house, there were three cruisers with two officers each. One of the vehicles had a police dog, as well. They were going to fan out around the property and they did another look inside the house.

The officer with the dog asked for a picture of Mattie, and an article of clothing he had recently worn. I worried that I didn't have anything that wasn't washed, but I did find his jacket he had on earlier. It was still hanging on the hook in the front hallway. I became even more worried when I saw that. Mattie was lost, and he didn't have his coat. 'Please dear God, let him be found before the sun goes down and it starts turning colder this evening."

When the officer passed the jacket in front of his dog's nose, the dog started going out of the driveway and towards the road.

One of the police cruisers started following them thinking that he may have wandered down the road. Ginger and Marmie tried to follow them, but we tried to hold them back. Did our dogs know where he went? Maybe the pup and Ginger tried to wander away or chase the truck this morning and Mattie ran after them. If so, he could be anywhere along the road or even picked up by someone. What if he was hit by a car, and left to die, or someone picked him up and taken him somewhere? My mind was going crazy over all the scenarios. All of them were scary thoughts and each one worse than another.

After the police had come, word had spread and some of our neighbors and people from our church came to our house. They all either helped search for him, prayed with us, or helped me with my other children. I was so distraught, and it helped having others with me.

We had searched for several hours, but this late in fall, the sun had set earlier than we would have liked. The temperature had dropped to thirty degrees after it became dark and everyone had started to go home for the night. I couldn't blame them, really. It was too difficult to search by night. So we thanked everyone and they promised to return the next morning. They said they wouldn't quit looking until he was found. I didn't want to give up the search, and I know I wouldn't get any sleep that night for worrying about my little boy.

CHAPTER 17

———— ❧ ————

JOSH AND MASON were not only deliverymen for the local lumberyard, but they were also best friends despite the difference in their ages. Mason was in his fifties and had worked for the company for years. He was the manager in the delivery department of the store. He was married and was a grandfather to children who were close in age to the Hoffman's children, and his youngest son had just finished high school this year. Josh was in his twenties and hadn't been working for the company for very long. This was his first job out of school. The delivery they made this day was the largest he had ever seen.

They were sitting in the break room at work talking about their day.

"Quite a load that we took to that Amish couple's place today, it totally wore me out. I'm going to be sore tomorrow," Mason said. "We don't often get so large an order."

"Actually, I believe they were Mennonites. You noticed they had a truck and a van in their yard, and they were dressed a tad different than the Amish," Josh replied.

"You seem to know a lot about them."

"I grew up around here, I had Amish and Mennonite friends in school. We hung out when they were doing their rumspringa. Those kids were crazy during that time. They had their first taste of freedom and boy did they take advantage of it. I thought regular kids were bad! Boy, howdy, we looked like saints compared to them!" Laughed Josh, as he reminisced. "After they got through running around, most of them decided to stay with their religion, though. I guess they decided freedom wasn't worth being shunned and never getting to speak to their families again and being outcasts from their way of life," Josh frowned.

"I guess that would be a hard choice to make for sure. Hey, speaking of running around, you up for going for a beer after we get off?" Mason asked.

"Sure, sounds good."

The store manager stepped into the break room while they were talking.

"You fellas, need to hose down the truck you took out today, so it will be clean and ready for the deliveries tomorrow. Looks like we have a couple more large orders. After you finish, you're free to leave."

They both looked at each other and groaned when they heard that tomorrow was going to be another heavy day.

The truck was a large flatbed truck suitable for carrying long wooden planks and other building materials. Now it was empty except for a large vinyl tarp that was laying in the back.

"Josh, you go turn the water on and I'll get the tarp off of it so it doesn't get wet."

"I think I left my jacket back there, too. Make sure you get that. It's getting a might nippy out here, I'd better put it on before we go much further and it accidently gets wet, too."

As Mason was pulling on the tarp to get it off the truck, something seemed to be holding it in place. He tugged, but it wouldn't budge.

"What the..." he frowned. He climbed up on the back of the truck to see where the tarp was hung up. "Are you kidding me?" He looked stunned.

Josh came around to the back of the truck after turning the water off.

"What's up boss?"

"Look at this." He pointed to a small boy lying there shivering and whimpering, and trying to stay warm.

"What is your name, little one?"

"Mattie."

"Just Mattie?" Josh asked.

"Yeth. I'm cold."

"Where did you come from?"

"I want to go home."

"Have you been back here all day?"

"Yeth, I want my mamma and dat."

Mason went into the store to get the manager and he came outside with him to see what all the commotion was about.

"Why didn't you bring him in the store where it's warm?"

"We just found him. I think he may have been out there most of the day."

"He looks cold and I'll bet he's hungry. Bring him inside so he can warm up and we'll get him a snack out of the machine. Then we'll call the police and they can sort it out. It seems like I remember seeing something on the news earlier about an Amber alert and a baby boy that was missing."

While the manager was phoning for the police, Josh bought a package of cupcakes from the vending machine and a bottled apple juice.

Mattie was sitting on the break room floor with a towel wrapped around him to warm him up and several layers of paper towels made into a makeshift diaper and taped with duct tape to replace his soaked and messed one that he had been wearing all day. His old dirty diaper was tossed out with the trash.

When the police officer arrived, they found Mattie with his mouth covered in chocolate and drinking some apple juice. He smiled when he saw the police officer. He seemed to remember him from the night of the fire.

"Mattie, go home," he whimpered.

"That's why we're here Mattie, to take you home." The officer pulled out the jacket they had gotten from the family earlier and slipped it on him.

"We just didn't know he was back there, officer, honest! He must have crawled under the tarp before we left the site. If our boss hadn't told us to hose the truck down, we probably wouldn't have found him until our next delivery tomorrow morning."

"Well, thank the Lord you listened to your boss! If he had to stay in below freezing temperatures over night, he wouldn't have made it until morning."

"So, are you ready to go home now, Mattie?" The officer asked as he picked him up.

"Yeth," he grinned.

"Your mamm and dat and sisters are going to be so happy to see you!" The officer smiled.

Since they didn't have an infant seat in the squad car, the deputy had to sit in the back seat of the cruiser and wrap the seatbelt around the two of them.

"This is kind of a tight fit, Mattie boy," the deputy smiled.

Mattie replied by nodding off to sleep and stayed that way all the way home.

Josh and Mason never went for that drink after work. Instead they decided to go home to their own wives and children.

Ben and I and the girls were deep in prayer for Mattie, while Luke slept, oblivious to the danger his older bruder was in. As I glanced at him, I thought; *'how wunderbaar it must be to not have a care in the world'.*

My heart leapt to my throat when I saw the flashing blue lights reflected on our wall. Ben still had his head bowed in prayer and didn't see them until I squeezed his hand and he lifted his eyes.

Why would the police have their blue lights on? Did they find Mattie? Was he okay? I prayed they weren't here to give us bad news.

The sheriff came to the door with his deputy behind him. I didn't see Mattie at first because he was asleep in his deputy's arms. When I saw the sheriff he was looking downcast.

"I'm sorry ma'am…"

My hand went to my throat and I thought I was going to pass out.

Then the sheriff added quickly: "I'm sorry, but you're going to have to call all your friends and neighbors tonight to cancel the search party tomorrow."

Then he grinned, and the deputy stepped out from behind him.

I didn't know what to think, Mattie was lying in his arms with something dark around his mouth that in the dim light looked like blood. I wondered if he had died and they were bringing his body home.

"Your little boy is going to be just fine. Sorry that was wrong of me to worry you," he apologized as the deputy placed him in my arms.

"What happened? Where was he?" Ben asked, after he recovered from the shock.

"Well, it seems that after the men from the lumberyard delivered your wood today, somehow your son climbed up on the back of the truck."

"How did we miss that, I wonder," Ben frowned.

"He might have done it while we were drinking coffee and settling the bill," I said.

"That could be. The kids were all running around playing around the wood boards. I just assumed that Matthew was with them, but why didn't we notice him on the back of the truck?" Ben asked.

"Maybe he was trying to hide or something. At any rate he more than likely was hiding under the tarp where you couldn't see him or even think to look for him there," the deputy suggested.

"Tonight the delivery men were getting ready to hose down the truck before they got off work and that's when they found him. They warmed him up and since they didn't have another diaper to put on him and he was soaked, they wrapped his bottom with paper towels. They got him some juice and a snack and then called us. We knew immediately that it was your son. I had his jacket from earlier, so I was able to put that on him, at least," the sheriff added.

"It's too bad that the men didn't check the truck earlier than tonight, but I'm glad they didn't wait until morning. This could've ended very badly," Ben frowned.

"You're right, Ben, but let's just thank God that it didn't happen."

After we signed off on all the paperwork from the police file, closing the case, we had a season of love with our children, especially Mattie. After I loved on him, I scolded him for running off and hiding and I told him how scared we were that we would never see him again.

"I'm sorry, Mamma," he said with tears in his eyes. "I won't do it again."

He looked so remorseful, I couldn't be angry with him. I was too busy wanting to love on him. I carried him upstairs to give him a bath and put some clean clothes on him. I had to laugh at the haphazard way the men covered his bottom with the paper towels. It looked really uncomfortable on him. I know he was happy to get the soft cloth ones on again.

After getting all the children to bed, it was too late to call everyone. I didn't want to disturb their family times. I decided we'd get up early and let everyone know that Matthew was home safe and sound. Maybe we'd catch them before they left their house in the morning. I didn't want them to make a trip for nothing. I did call Linda and John because I didn't want them to stay awake and worry about us.

After the stressful day, we fell into bed and slept soundly through the night. When I woke up, the rooster was announcing the morning. I walked over to Luke's bed and wondered why I hadn't heard him all night.

I was relieved when I saw him squirming around in his cradle waiting on me to change his diaper and feed him.

While I was taking care of him, Ben saw to the other children, getting them up and feeding them. They decided that they wanted cereal for breakfast and I was thankful that I didn't have to stop everything to cook for them.

I heard voices coming from outside. "Ach, we didn't get up soon enough to call everyone. Although they'll be glad to hear that Mattie has been found, they'll be upset that they made their way here and took time out of their busy lives for nothing."

After I was dressed I went out to greet our friends and saw our picnic table covered with all kinds of snacks and goodies. I guess the women thought that we were going to have a long day searching for Mattie and wanted to bring sustenance for everyone.

They all came up to me and hugged me when they heard the news that he had been found.

I heard one of the men call out to the others, "While we're here we might as well get some work done!"

The rest of the men agreed.

"How many hammers and saws you got, Ben?" another called out.

"A few, what do you need them for?" Ben called back to him.

"Looks, like we have enough folk here to begin this barn raising!"

"You don't have to do this, you've helped us so much already by looking for our son."

"You know you'd do the same for us, Ben," Zeke said. "This is just what the folks do around here. Besides, the sooner you get this barn built and get your life back in order, the sooner you'll be able to help get our business going. Christmas is coming soon and I have a ton of orders. I'm going to be needing your help."

Ben laughed, "Well, as long as you put it that way."

With everyone working together, it didn't take too many days to finish the barn. It was larger and better than the old one. Two weeks later, after the barn was started, we were able to bring all our animals back. Once they were returned, we bought several bags of feed from the local feed store to supplement the grain that we were able to salvage from the fire. Thankfully, we had some hay still in the fields and in another outside storage building, that wasn't touched by the fire. It looked like, between all of it, we had enough to get us through the winter.

Ben wanted to get the barn painted before the bad weather started, but he didn't quite get to it in time. After he finished off the inside and made it habitable for the animals, we had our first blizzard of the winter.

C H A P T E R   1 8

Winter

PEOPLE WHO LIVED in our area thought I was crazy because I really enjoyed the winter. Being as I grew up in the south central part of North Carolina, I didn't see too much snow. We had the occasional snowstorm, but it melted off a day or two later or we had an ice storm that was more of a nuisance than anything. I've been in Pennsylvania going on seven years now, and I was still not tired of the brisk weather and the beautiful snowfalls. Of course, if I had to get out in it everyday to drive to work, I would probably feel differently about it. Living at home and being a farmer's wife and a stay at home mamm had its perks when it came to weather like this.

The downside of this weather was that we still had to go outside and trudge through the snow to get to the barn and take care of all the animals, and the livestock wasn't able to get out and exercise and eat the fresh green grass they so dearly loved.

Ben had enough foresight to build some heating elements into the barn so that the animals wouldn't get too cold, but it wasn't ever warm enough that they would get so use to the heat that they would refuse to go outside in the cold weather.

All the children loved playing in the snow. Deidre showed Anna and Matthew how to make snow angels. I worried about Matthew getting too wet or cold, even though he seemed perfectly healthy now. I was afraid that something else would happen to him. I guess I was just overly protective because of his history.

Mattie was scheduled to go back to the EENT doctor for his six-month check-up because of his ear-tubes. The doctor just wanted to see if they were still in place, which, of course, they were.

Luke was three months old now, and was the size of a full grown newborn baby. The doctor declared him to be completely healthy, and at a normal weight at his last checkup. After all the worries about me being exposed to measles, it was a relief to hear.

Deidre, or Deedee, as we nicknamed her, was Mamma's little helper. She loved her younger siblings and watched over them while I was busy at the cook stove or doing the dishes or laundry. She even helped me make the dolls and baby quilts that we would soon sell in Sarah's and my gift shop. She seemed to have a real knack for needlecrafts. She seemed so grown up for a five year old. I dreaded the day that she would start school and I didn't have her around most of the day. I guess her mother's helper mantle would have to pass on to her little sister when that day came.

Anna had just turned four and was getting as grown up acting as her big sister. She and Deedee were inseparable most of the time. They were close in age and were best friends, at least until they met Rebekah and Rachel, Sarah and Zeke's twin daughters. They were the same age as Anna and she often felt jealous when her older sister tried to horn in on them while they played.

Now that our husbands were going to work together, Sarah and I became great friends. We were looking forward to starting our business together. When the weather and roads cooperated, we were often at each other's houses. While the children played and Luke napped or entertained himself, we would make a pot of tea and drink from Grandy Dee's teacups and discuss how we wanted to set up our business and plan menus for the tearoom part of it. We would often spend the time making items to sell.

While we were discussing the shop, the men would be working on some furniture pieces. Ben surprised me one day when he brought in a brand new baby crib for Luke. It was beautiful! He made a dressing table for him to match. It could eventually be converted into a dresser for when he was older. Luke had started to outgrow his cradle that was still in our bedroom, so it was good that he had his own crib now. It was to be put in the same room as his older brother. I just hoped they wouldn't keep each other awake at night.

Thanksgiving was quickly coming upon us and we received a call from my parents saying that they were planning to come up for a visit. It had been over a year since we last saw them. They had never met our newest baby and Matthew was about Luke's age when they were last here. My stepsister-in-law, Kari, and her family were planning on coming with them. I heard they were planning on renting a large van so they all could make it in one vehicle. Kari's children, Aiden and Laurie, were young teenagers now. They were only children when they were in our wedding. It seemed hard to believe they were almost adults now.

My parents would be staying with us, while Kari and Jacob and their children would stay with Linda and John.

In thinking back on her history, I was glad that Kari had been reunited with her mamm after being separated for so many years because of a misunderstanding over religion, or lack of it, by Kari. Now, even though Kari's family didn't belong to the Mennonite faith of her mamm and stepfather, they were strong Christians in their own church back home, and she was on good terms with them. Ben met his older stepsister just a few years before we met and the two of them hit it off from the very beginning. It was like they had known each other their whole lives.

When Ben and I had done some research into his stepmother's background during the summer I met him, we learned that his mamm was actually my great grandmother's granddaughter, So, my stepmother-in-law was also a cousin to my mamm, and Kari, besides being a stepsister-in-law, was also some sort of cousin to me. It was complicated.

A few days before Thanksgiving, we had a break in the weather. The skies cleared and the temperatures were warm enough to melt the snows from the blizzard we had the week before.

It was nice to be able to open the windows and air out the rooms before our guests arrived. I had started to do some baking and then put what I had made in the freezer for the holidays so I wouldn't have so much to do when they arrived, and would have more time to enjoy our visit.

Ben decided to go ahead and get as much painting done on the barn as he could so it would be winterized before the rest of the winter hit us full force. It took a few days, but between him and Caleb, they managed to finish it. It looked so beautiful with its new coat of red paint.

All of the animals seemed happy to be able to go into the fields again and even managed to find some blades of grass through the melting snow.

After the barn was painted, we gave Caleb some time off, so he could go home and visit his family. He needed some vacation time away from us, especially after the year we had, but we had another reason for doing this. He was staying in our guest room, and we needed it for my parents.

After he left, even though he was a model boarder and kept his room fairly clean, I had a chance to clean his room further from top to bottom and put out clean sheets and a fresh quilt for them.

While I was cleaning, Anna ran into the room, "Mamma, Mamma, Dawdy and Mammi Edgerton are here!"

I ran to the window and saw them getting out of the van. Ben and the girls were hugging them and blocking their way when they were trying to get to the house. They all looked so happy to be reunited. Mattie held back and acted bashful, as he really didn't know them, but I knew all that would change, especially since they brought presents for each of them. That was a sure way to win them over.

I met them at the door because I didn't want to get out in the cool air with Luke. Dad and Ben took the suitcases up the stairs to the guest room.

"Samantha you look terrific," my mother said. "Being a mother and farmer's wife has certainly agreed with you."

I smiled at her. "Yes, but it's not been very easy, and this past year has taken a lot out of me, of us, with everything we've been through, but I've tried to hold it together. Ben and his parents have been terrific."

"I'm sorry we couldn't have helped more, but it would've been impossible for your dad and I to get our work schedules coordinated and it is such a long drive up here."

"That's alright, Mamm, like I said everyone's been great. We have a lot of friends and neighbors who were willing to help out too."

"I'm glad we were at least able to help you out when Matthew was in the hospital."

"What do you mean?"

"We paid his hospital bill, of course."

"I didn't know that. They told us the donation was anonymous. We just figured it was someone at our church who paid it. I had no idea you all did. Thank you so much. It really helped out a lot! Especially with everything else that happened after that."

"You all seem to be doing okay now."

"We are okay, the Lord has gotten us through all our trials and we are stronger for having gone through them."

"Has your husband ever started working?"

"Well, he hadn't really looked, you do realize he's a farmer, right? That is his job."

"He can't possibly make all that much doing that. What do you live on? How can you raise four children on what he makes?"

In the course of our conversation, I realized why I never missed my parents all that much. I just hoped I could bite my tongue from saying something I would later regret.

"We are actually doing very well. The way we live, we don't require much. The house is paid for and I make our own clothes and we grow our own food. We sell food and crafts at the local market every weekend and that pays for our incidentals and utilities. Ben and I are actually going to join this Amish family, who are friends of ours, in a business venture come this spring. Ben is going to start helping him build furniture and his wife and I are going to run the shop."

"That should help some, as long as you all don't have to invest much in it."

"Only in supplies, but we should get our money back and a profit to boot. Besides, I think it will be a lot of fun. We're even going to run a tearoom in the shop."

"You might want to talk with Kari about that. You have no idea how much work it is to try to keep one going."

"You're not very encouraging."

"Just being realistic, dear. But I do hope it turns out well for you. Maybe this will help."

Just then she handed me an envelope.

"What's this?" I asked her.

"Oh, Samantha, I didn't want to have to tell you this, especially with the holidays and our visit together, but with all the struggles you've been going through, there wasn't ever a good time to let you know about your grandmother."

"What happened?"

"A few months ago she had another massive stroke and this time she didn't make it."

"Oh no, I'm so sorry, I didn't know."

"How could you have, I didn't tell anyone, not even her brother and sister."

"Uncle Freddie, and Aunt Jessica didn't know? Does Ben's parents know?"

"No, honey, no one knew."

"That's sad that she died alone. Was there anyone at her funeral?"

"Just some people who knew her from the nursing home and us, of course."

"Mamm, how could you not tell anyone? That was just wrong!" I felt very angry when I lashed out at her, and wanted to immediately take it back. This was going to be a very long week while they were staying with us, for sure and for certain.

"I'm sorry, Samantha, I should have told you, but like I said, you were having enough troubles without worrying about this, too. Your grandmother was very sick and it was only a matter of time before she had another stroke. There wasn't anything anyone could do. She didn't even know us the last time we visited her. Anyway, there is some money in that envelope. There wasn't a lot left of her inheritance after paying off her debts at the nursing home, but in her will she wanted to include you and us. We wanted to deliver the money to you personally so we would make sure you got it."

I opened the envelope, and there was a cashier's check for twenty-five thousand dollars. The amount stunned me. I had no idea that she had that kind of money. But then again, when I thought back to her life, I remembered what Grandy Dee told me about her. How she and her husband were war correspondents and how he had lost his leg because of a land mine while they were covering a story and then he was killed in the attack on the World Trade Center on 9/11. She must have gotten some money from settlements from those two things.

"Thank you for bringing this, Mamm, I appreciate it, I really do, but I'm still upset with you for not telling me about her death."

"I was wrong to keep it from you. I'm sorry."

After that, we hugged and I forgave her. I know she was just trying to spare me any further heartache at the time I was already overburdened with my own problems.

The day before Thanksgiving, Ben and my father went hunting for a turkey. There was a special reserve close by that specialized in raising turkeys so the men in the area could hunt for their own. I wasn't sure how my city slicker father would do with that. Especially when it came to dressing it for our meal. We were use to plucking our own chickens, and even our children had gotten use to it, but I wasn't sure how he would handle all the blood and stripping it down.

While they were out hunting, Mamm helped me in the kitchen making desserts for the next day and we took turns chasing after the children and watching out for baby Luke.

That evening Kari and her family came to our house for supper.

It was great to see them again and I was especially interested in talking with Kari about her tearoom. It had been over seven years since I worked with her and I was anxious to find out how it was going, especially after what my mother said about her.

After we ate, the girls went off to play with Laurie, and Mattie stayed close to us, wanting attention. I think he was feeling left out of the big kids games. Aiden went outside to be with the men to watch them finish cleaning the turkeys.

"When will Lukie be old enough to play, Mamma?" Mattie frowned.

"Not until he can walk around on his own, honey. It will be a few months."

I found him a coloring book and sat him in the booster chair so he could sit at the table with us. Kari, Mamm, and I had a cup of tea with our dessert and visited while Dat, Jacob, Ben, and Aiden were out in the barn. They managed to kill two turkeys that day, so it would take a little while to clean both of them. I would cook one for our dinner tomorrow and I would send the other one to Ben's parents for their dinner.

Kari and I talked about the plans that Sarah and I had for our gift shop and tearoom. Kari was very enthusiastic about it and thought it was a wonderful idea. She said that she loved working at her restaurant, but it was getting so popular, especially after the article in the tea magazine, that she could barely keep up with it anymore, and at times she would get burned out with it. "At least your place won't be quite so hectic and you have a gift shop to go with it, so you won't be doing the same thing all the time. Plus, you're going to be running it with your best friend. As long as the two of you get along, it shouldn't be a problem."

"Jah, I can't wait. I think it will be gut."

"So who's going to watch the children while you two are working?"

"We are going to take turns with them. They will have a playroom in the back."

"That sounds like it will work out as long you don't get too busy. You might want to see about hiring a girl to help out, though. Better to be safe, than sorry."

"You're probably right. We'll see how it goes. It will take a few months to get it up and running, and then we'll have to build up our customer base. I honestly don't know how busy we'll be."

"You might be surprised. I didn't think my tearoom would do much, but we can hardly keep up with the demand now," Kari grinned. "Once your name is out there, you're going to be the hotspot for the locals, as well as the tourists."

About that time, the men came in from the barn, dirty and bloody from dressing the turkeys.

"Ach, you better go wash up, you all are a mess!" I frowned.

After they cleaned up, Jacob came back to the kitchen. "We better get the kids and head back to your mom's house. They'll think we got lost and I could use a real bath. I'll tell you what, from now on we'll just get our turkeys from the grocery stores like normal people," he laughed.

"But ours will taste better, knowing everything we had to do to bring it to the table," Ben grinned. "This is how the pilgrims did it after all."

"I'm sure," Jacob winked. "We'd better get going don't want our bird to spoil before we get it to Linda and John's house."

After settling the children down for bed. My parents sat down with us while we did our evening devotional. I was surprised that they wanted to participate and they seemed to really enjoy it.

We visited for a short while, catching up on things that had been happening in our lives since the last time we seen each other.

"So do you have any plans for what you're going to do with the money?" Mamm asked.

"What money?" Ben looked at me with a questioning look in his eye.

"I haven't had the chance to tell you with everything that's been going on today. Mamm gave me some sad news today while you all were out. It seems my grandmother, Anna, passed away from a stroke a few months back and she left us some money in her will. My parents brought a cashiers check for twenty-five thousand dollars for us."

"You are just now hearing about this?" Ben asked, incredulously.

"We didn't want to add to all of the problems you were having at that time, Ben," my father added.

"We could have handled it. We're stronger than you think," Ben frowned.

"I apologize for our short-sightedness. We both see that now," my father continued.

"So what are you going to do with the money?" My mother asked again.

"Obviously we haven't thought anything about it yet, but more than likely we'll put it aside in a savings account, and use it towards our new business as needs arise and for any other emergencies that may come up."

After talking for a little while longer we decided to get settled down for the night. It had been a long day and everyone seemed tired. The next day was Thanksgiving. Our family and my parents would have our main dinner here, and Linda and John would have their dinner with Kari and Jacob, but in the evening we planned all get together as one large family and share our leftovers with each another.

My father was lamenting the fact that he missed his overstuffed easy chair and television to watch the football games after Thanksgiving dinner, but my mother told him he could get over it for one year, but then she complained that she would be missing the black Friday sales the next day. I had to laugh at them. How did I ever grow up in the world where those things were more important than family togetherness and being thankful to God during these holidays?

The day after Thanksgiving my parents planned on leaving so they could get back home before the storm that was forecast for the weekend moved in.

They wanted to get an early start in the morning so they could go by and pick up Kari and Jacob at my in-law's house and then leave from there.

Even though they gave me moments of displeasure at times while they were here, I knew I would miss them. We only got to see each other about once every year or two and it was hard to say goodbye to them this time for some reason. Maybe it was because I saw the tears in my children's eyes as they hugged them and told them they loved them and were going to miss them.

I wish I could've said goodbye to my sister-in-law and her family, but after my parents left we had to get our chores done. The storm they had predicted was moving in more quickly than they had originally forecasted, so we were rushing around to make sure all of the animals were gathered and sheltered back in the barn.

Our Indian summer was over and the cold wave moved in around lunchtime. I prayed my parents would keep ahead of it since it was moving in their direction. If they were making good time, they should have been about half way home by now.

CHAPTER 19

LATER THAT AFTERNOON, Caleb came back to the farm. We didn't expect him until the next day, but he wanted to make sure we had all the animals taken care of and returned to the barn, and there was enough wood chopped to last for several days if we were to lose power and have to resort to cooking on the woodstove and heating the house with the fireplaces. Ach, maybe I didn't like the winter as much as I thought I did.

The children were excited about the snow and begged me to go out and play with them and they even talked me into making snow ice cream later.

I bundled the three of them up and warned them with a stern warning to not leave the sight of their dat.

After nursing Luke and changing his diaper, I got him down for a nap and then I set about redding the guest room back for Caleb. I honestly don't know why we still had him staying with us since our intruder was no longer a problem, but it was nice having an extra hand around to help Ben with his work. It would be even more important when Ben started working with Ezekiel Beiler. John said that we could keep him as long as we needed, because Jeremiah was such a good worker that he didn't think he needed Caleb that much anymore.

Later in the evening, the men came in carrying armloads of chopped wood for the fireplaces.

"Mrs. Hoffman, we could sure use a cup of hot cocoa when we get through. It is getting mighty cold out there."

"Sure, I'll get the water heated. Would you tell Ben to bring the children in? They've been out there long enough."

Later, we sat and had our cocoa and ate some turkey sandwiches and pumpkin pie to go along with it. It was the first time I really had the chance to sit and talk with Caleb since he returned to us.

"So, Caleb, how was your family doing? Did you enjoy your visit home?" I asked.

"It was good. My mamm and dat decided to adopt this thirteen-year-old girl. She's been in and out of foster homes for seven years. My parents have had her for the past year and the state finally gave their approval for her adoption. I felt kind of sorry for her. Her life was so sad. She was six years old when she was first taken over by the state. She's been pretty torn up about everything that she went through."

"What happened to her parents?" I asked, wondering if she could have been Danny's daughter.

"She watched as her mother died in childbirth and then her dat went to prison for trying to kill someone."

"Caleb, her name wouldn't be Cecilia would it?"

"Yes, that's it! Why do you ask?"

"You know that man that tried to kill Ben? He was the same man who attacked him seven years ago and torched his truck."

"You know, I remember what he said that night of the fire. You don't reckon he heard about his daughter staying at my folk's house and came here looking for me so he could get to his daughter, do you?" Caleb asked.

"That actually makes sense, when you put it that way. He might have been looking for her and when he saw Deedee, thought that he could use her as leverage to get his daughter back," Ben said.

"I guess that's why, after her father's death, she became available to be adopted. I just didn't put two and two together. That means, he could have been looking to get me and not you!" Caleb exclaimed.

"Or he was looking for me out of revenge for my testimony against him that put him behind bars to start with," Ben frowned.

"Ach, whatever it was, it's over now, thank goodness. Caleb, you'll have to bring Cecilia over sometime. We'd like to meet her and get to know her better," I said.

"Just don't let her know, or remind her that I'm the one responsible for her dat's imprisonment and that it was our barn that he was killed in," Ben added.

"I don't believe that she's anyone who would try and get revenge. She's actually pretty nice and she's aware that her father did some bad things, so I don't believe she'd hold it against you. She even told us one time that her dat use to beat her mamm and her. She was really afraid of him. I almost believe she was glad when he was killed."

My heart went out to this girl who I had never met. What a tragic life for someone so young. I thanked God everyday for the relationship I had with my husband and our beautiful children who would always know what it meant to have loving parents. I prayed that with Caleb's family she would finally learn what it liked to be loved.

Later that evening my parents finally called, saying they arrived back home okay. They said there were a few icy patches and heavy snow in places and they were almost in a wreck a few times, but they finally made it home in one piece after dropping Kari and her family off at their house.

After Thanksgiving was over, it was time to think about Christmas. When I was growing up, my mother and I would head out to the mall at all hours in the morning to beat everyone else for the best buys the day after Thanksgiving. Here, we didn't buy any store bought decorations or gifts, but we preferred to make our own. We even made homemade Christmas cards to send out. The girls loved to help with those. When the children were asleep or outside playing, I worked on a few things for them as a surprise on Christmas day. I made all of them a teddy bear, and for the girls, a new doll with different clothes they could change them into, and a quilt for their dolls. Ben made the girls a small cradle for their new dolls, and he made Matthew a wagon large enough to give his dog, Marmalade, a ride. I knitted new mittens and sweaters for everyone, including Ben. But the biggest surprise for the children was coming from their dat. He bought a new pony and riding equipment to be delivered on Christmas Eve after the children were in bed. I couldn't wait for them to see it!

We didn't have a Christmas tree or elaborate decorations around the house, but closer to Christmas we would gather some pine branches and place them on the mantles of the fireplaces and on the tables and we made wreaths to put in the windows. We liked to put candles in the windows and on the table along with the greenery to give the house a warm and welcome feel about it. We would place our homemade ornaments throughout the garlands of pine. I loved the smell and feel of our humble, homemade Christmas decorations. After living in the secular and over-commercialized Christmases back home while I was growing up, I really appreciated this simpler way of doing things. It just seemed like it was a better alternative.

In our religion, Christ was the most important part of Christmas. After the children received their gifts on Christmas morning, the rest of the day was a celebration of Jesus's birth. We had a special service at church and the children would act out a Christmas play. Then the pastor would give everyone a candy cane and tell them the legend of the candy. He explained that it was white and red, because the purity of

Christ was the white part and the red because of his blood he shed for our sins and the candy was shaped like a 'J' because in one direction it was the first letter of his name, and the other direction it was shaped like a shepherds staff, because he was the good shepherd. Such a simple story and the children loved it and they loved getting the candy too.

Another part of our Christmas that I loved was joining some of the rest of our congregation in going Christmas caroling. We would ride around in horse drawn buggies and sing and hand out packets of home-made cookies to everyone. It was so much fun.

On Christmas morning, the children came running down the stairs when they smelled the warm cinnamon rolls that I just finished baking for our breakfast. It was their favorite and I only made them for special occasions. Ben was sitting at the table guarding their treasures waiting for them in the basins they sat out the night before. We had a tablecloth spread over their gifts so they couldn't peak until we were all together and could enjoy their reaction when they saw their presents. Besides the gifts we had made, there was also some store bought candy. They didn't normally get candy, so this was an extra special treat for them.

After eating their breakfast and exploring all of the things in their basins, Ben told them, as he winked at me, "We need to go out to the barn, because even though it's Christmas, we still have chores to do."

After some pretty obvious groans, the children did as they were told and ran to get their jackets and put their new mittens and hats on. When we got to the porch, they stopped and stared. Sitting on the porch was Mattie's new red, wooden wagon and the girls' new doll beds. Each of them had a down mattress and pillow and quilt that were a perfect doll size. They all three hugged the two of us, thanking us for their wunderbaar presents.

Ben looked at the children more sternly and shook his finger at them. "You can play with these after your chores are done. We need to go take care of the animals first, understand?"

"Yes, Dat," they all said in unison, frowning.

I hung back a little from them, wrapping Luke a little tighter in his blanket against the cold December air. We made our way to the barn where their final Christmas present was revealed.

"I think we need to take care of the horses first of all," he smiled. "They need their Christmas oats, jah?"

"Can we give them a sugar cube for Christmas, Dat?" asked Anna.

"Sure, that's a gut idea. They will like that," he replied.

They walked into the stables and stopped.

"Where did this horse come from?" Deedee asked.

"Merry Christmas, children!" Ben and I exclaimed.

"This pony is for all of you, so you'll have to share and take turns riding him, and you are also going to have to learn to take care of him. That will be all your responsibilities, okay?"

"Jah, thank you Dat and Mamma," Deedee replied.

"We love him! Best Christmas ever," Anna chimed in.

Matthew walked over to the pony and hugged his hind leg, the only part he could put his arms around.

"Son, first thing you need to learn is not to get too close to his back end until you get to know him. You don't want him to get spooked and kick you."

"Okay, Dat," he said, as he backed away.

"Can we ride him now, Dat?" Anna asked.

"Maybe after dinner, remember we're going to Mammi and Dawdy's house to visit and eat our dinner with them. We don't need to get too messy before we go," I reminded them.

It was chilly outside, so the girls and I went back into the house. They carried in their new doll beds and spent the rest of the morning playing with their dolls and dressing them in the different clothes I made for them. They wanted to find just the right outfit to put on them for their trip to Mammi and Dawdy's house.

Matthew was outside following his dat around while he was feeding and taking care of the animals. He somehow managed to coax Marmalade into the wagon and was pulling him up and down the pathway between the porch and the barn, the only part of the yard that wasn't covered with snow. The dog was nearly fully grown at six months, and Mattie was almost two. They were nearly the same size. It was comical watching him trying to pull the wagon over the rough ground with the heavy dog as his passenger. The next time I looked out the window I smiled as I saw Ben pulling a very happy Mattie around in it and Marmalade patiently watching him and waiting for his turn again.

Christmas dinner at my in-laws was as delicious as I expected it would be. She baked a ham, and made mashed potatoes and a green bean casserole, and fresh homemade dinner rolls and I brought the desserts.

The children chattered on relentlessly about their new toys and candy, and especially about their new pony that they couldn't wait to get home to.

"Now children, there will be time for that, but right now let's enjoy this delicious dinner that your mamma, and mammi worked so hard to make for us, jah?' Ben scolded.

Later that day, the children finally did get to take turns on the pony and afterwards we went to church for the Christmas program.

I was pleasantly surprised when I saw so many at church, including the policeman who we shared our faith with following the attack on Ben. He told us that he had been doing a lot of thinking about what happened to us, and our reaction to the intruder that tried to kill Ben. He wanted to learn more about God and his saving grace and why we had so much faith in something that was beyond comprehension. He seemed to be moved by the service and promised that he and his family would be back to visit again soon. He said he wanted to learn more about our religion, and maybe eventually join our faith community.

We were thankful, that we no longer needed his services, at least anytime soon. It would be nice to someday welcome him and his wife into our home as a brother and sister in the Lord and not as someone who was there to get us out of trouble.

Maybe, if because of what happened to our family this year, one person was brought to God through our troubles, just maybe it was worth it after all.

Epilogue

THE REST OF the winter was relatively calm. Other than a few minor sniffles that went along with the cold weather and being cooped up in the house most of the time, we seemed to fair well during those months.

Ben did most of the outside work when the weather permitted. I was glad that he put a little warmth into the new barn with the built-in heaters that he installed when he built the barn so while he was caring for the animals he wouldn't be so cold. He took Matthew with him to the barn most days. Mattie wanted to be with his dat, 'doing man's work', as he would say. Ginger and Marmalade stayed right with him to keep him out of trouble. I was glad because, goodness knows, he's seen his fair share of problems this year.

The girls spent most of their days helping me in the kitchen and taking care of baby Luke. They were wonderful caregivers to him. I think they thought of him as their own little baby doll.

Their cat, Mittens, was still around and as spoiled as ever. Most of the time she could be seen curled up in one of the doll beds, asleep with them. We kept her in the house during the cold weather, but when the weather turned warmer, I knew she'd be ready to go back outside. Soon, she would be needed as a mouser as we start to harvest our crops next year and store them in the barn, but I let the girls have their time with her as long as possible right now, since they enjoy her so much. I just hope that when it comes time to let her out to stay in the barn, she will want to leave the comfort of the house.

It had been over six months since Mattie had his ear tubes put in and at the last follow up visit with the doctor, he noticed that the tubes finally did come out on their own, and his eardrums had healed. I was glad that it happened that way rather than putting him through the trauma of having them removed surgically.

Deidre's burns healed up nicely with no residual scarring. Physically, she was doing great, but mentally, it still remained to be seen. I know I still have nightmares of the fire and her being taken hostage, I can't imagine the horror and pain she felt as she was being held at gunpoint against her will and then being burned. It was bound to affect her some way.

Anna, my dear sweet younger daughter managed to get by this year without anything bad happening to her. She was fortunate, but as life goes on, I'm sure she'll eventually get into some kind of scrapes, but I know God will protect her, as he has the rest of us, if anything were to ever happen to her.

When Ben finished his daily chores around the farm, he often made his way over to Zeke's house. Zeke had an area in his barn that was set up to do his carpentry work. I think Ben was a tad bit jealous of all of his equipment. I'm sure it won't be long before Ben has a place set up of his own, too. In the meantime they spent part of their days together building things to put in our shop when we eventually do get it opened.

Sometimes the children and I went with Ben to their house. Sarah and I spent the afternoons together working on our crafts and needle-work to sell in the store. We wanted to have a good supply when we open it later in the spring.

While we were working on our projects, the kinner kept each other company. It was so nice to have someone their age to be friends with. The girls played together and often left Mattie out of it. He wasn't too interested in keeping up with his sisters and their friends. He often made his way to the workshop in their barn to be with his dat and Zeke. They let him play with the scrap pieces of wood and let him build things out of them.

One day, when the weather warmed up, we were driving around and spotted an old house that was for sale along the main road. It was a real fixer-upper, but it was in a good location and looked perfect for our little shop. It wasn't real big, but it had a large front room and a separate dining room. There were two upstairs bedrooms that we'd be able to use for storage and a makeshift daycare for the children. We went to Ezekiel and Sarah and told them about it. Later, they stopped by to look at it and fell in love with it, as well.

We contacted the real estate agent and put in an offer on it right on the spot. We knew it probably wouldn't pass an inspection in the condition it was in, but we didn't have any worries. By the time we finished fixing it up, it would be perfect.

Over the next few months, my life would become even more complicated. Between raising four children, being a farmer's wife with everything that involved, working on projects to sell, helping getting the new shop ready to be opened at the beginning of summer and then working in it as a sales person, I didn't think I could handle many more projects or problems, but God had other plans for my friends and us. Plans that no one could have ever imagined.

While I was growing up, I would sometimes read stories about the Amish and Mennonite people. I guess I was interested because my great grandmother was one. The stories sounded so nice and their lives sounded so uncomplicated and peaceful. Others, who only had a cursory knowledge of their life, would even refer to them as being 'plain' and 'simple'.

When I fell deeply in love and married Benjamin Hoffman seven years ago, I expected my life to be this idyllic existence that I read about in the novels, but the reality was so very different. Not that I would give up my life for anything in the world, nor trade with any other woman that I know of, but my life has ended up being anything but 'plain' and 'simple'.

Afterward

Watch for the continuing saga of Samantha Hoffman and her friends in my new series:

Women of God: Lancaster County

To get more of the background story of Samantha and her family, be sure to read my book
"Tea with Grandy Dee"

Author Bio

ALTHOUGH DEANNA STALNAKER'S writing career didn't begin until she retired from nursing in 2013, she always had dreams of being an author. Immediately following that cold November day when she left her "real" job, she started giving away her uniforms and invested in a good computer and printer. Now two years later, she has written and published ten books and is working on more. The first series of books she wrote was her "Women of God " novels. Then came a devotional book and children's book. All of her books are based on her love of God and the Bible and what it teaches us for a better life. In her novels, there is also an echo of her former life as a nurse, as many of her protagonists, their friends, or their families have some types of medical emergencies.

She is currently living in North Carolina with her husband and one of their two daughters, who also is a writer.

www.ingramcontent.com/pod-product-compliance
Lightning Source LLC
Chambersburg PA
CBHW070836120626
46556CB00002B/775